Ancestral Lines

To Sevy, with love.

Chapter 1

The golden hues of the evening sun bathed the vineyards in a warm glow as Jean-Pierre Dupont leaned against the fence, watching Giselle and Pascal dart between the rows of grapevines. Their laughter echoed through the still air, blending with the rustling of leaves. With her boundless energy, Giselle charged ahead, while Pascal, always a step behind, followed her lead, giggling and mimicking her every move.

Jean-Pierre smiled, his mind drifting back to his childhood. He could almost see himself and Chantelle running through those same vineyards, their laughter as carefree and uninhibited as the wind. He remembered how they'd race each other, rolling on the soft grass when they tumbled, their clothes stained with dirt and grape juice. Chantelle would tease him mercilessly when he lost, and he'd retaliate by chasing her until they were both out of breath, collapsing side by side under the shade of the ancient oak tree.

His father, Marcel, would often call them in with a chuckle, shaking his head at their antics but secretly delighted by their joy. Marcel told them stories then—of his childhood spent in the vineyard and of Jean-Pierre's grandfather, who had toiled tirelessly on the same land.

Marcel often recounted how he and his siblings would play hide-and-seek among the vines when they weren't helping their father with the harvest. The stories painted vivid pictures in Jean-Pierre's young mind, making him feel part of something timeless and profound.

Now, watching his children frolic in those same rows, Jean-Pierre felt a deep connection. It was as if history was repeating itself, a never-ending cycle of joy and work, love and legacy. He wondered how many generations of Dupont's had run, played, and laughed in these vineyards.

Jean-Pierre called out to the children as the sun dipped lower, casting long shadows across the fields. "Giselle, Pascal, time to head in!"

Giselle squealed in protest but grabbed her brother's hand, pulling him along as they raced back to their father. Jean-Pierre scooped up Pascal, his son's face smudged with dirt and his hands sticky from clutching overripe grapes. Giselle grabbed his free arm, beaming up at him with her wide, toothy grin.

"You two look like you've been rolling in the dirt all day," Jean-Pierre teased as he carried them towards the house.

"We were working, *Papa*!" Giselle said proudly. "We were helping in the vineyard!"

"Oh, is that so?" Jean-Pierre chuckled. "Well, you're dirty enough to convince me."

They stepped into the warm, inviting kitchen, where Ana stood at the counter, humming as she prepared dinner. She turned to greet them, her laughter ringing out when she saw the children's state.

"What have they been up to this time?" Ana asked, shaking her head with amused exasperation.

Jean-Pierre set Pascal down and put an arm around Giselle. "Oh, you know, just toiling the land like all the Duponts before them," he said with a wink.

Ana laughed, wiping her hands on a dish towel. "Is that right? Starting them early, are we?"

Jean-Pierre leaned against the counter, his expression softening. "It makes you think, though," he said. "How many generations have done this? Marcel used to tell me stories about his father and how he worked the land. And I wondered if there were other Dupont children, long before us, playing in these rows just like Giselle and Pascal."

Ana smiled; her eyes warm with understanding. "It's a beautiful thought," she said. "Growing up in the country, surrounded by all this... it's the best childhood they could have. My sister and I used to play hide-and-seek in the fields, just like this. We'd come home filthy, and *Maman* would scold us while secretly smiling."

Jean-Pierre grinned. "Then you understand why I let them run wild."

Just then, the sound of a car pulling into the driveway caught their attention. Moments later, Aunty Chantelle stepped into the kitchen, still in her scrubs. Her face lit up when she saw the children, and they rushed to greet her, shouting, "*Tata* Chantelle!"

"What have you two been up to?" Chantelle asked, crouching down to hug them. "Has your dad put you to work in the vineyards already?"

Jean-Pierre laughed. "You know me, starting them young."

Giselle clambered onto Chantelle's lap; her face animated as she recounted their day. "We ran through the grapes, *Tata* Chantelle. And *Papa* couldn't catch us!"

Pascal giggled, nodding vigorously. "*Papa* couldn't catch us!"

Chantelle laughed, holding one child on each knee. "Sounds like you two are faster than your old man. But don't tell him I said that."

Jean-Pierre leaned against the counter, watching the three of them. "You know," he said, his tone thoughtful, "I wonder how many Duponts before us played in those rows, Chantelle. How many generations laughed and ran just like we did?"

Chantelle looked up at him, her smile softening. "Probably more than we could ever imagine," she said. "But it doesn't really matter, does it? What matters is that it's happening again, right here, right now." Jean-Pierre nodded, his heart full.

Later, Chantelle led the children upstairs for their baths, their giggles echoing down the hallway. When she returned, Giselle and Pascal were scrubbed clean, dressed in fresh pyjamas, and ready for dinner.

As the family sat down to eat, laughter and stories filled the room, binding them together in the unbroken thread of love, legacy, and the simple joy of being together.

Mario Zatta

Chapter 2

J ean-Pierre was up bright and early. As usual, he woke up as the sun rose. He loved this time of the morning, the fresh new rays of sun warming up the land, the sound of the wind rustling the leaves, and the birds starting their songs. He loved the freshness, the dew-soaked leaves of the vineyards, and the crisp smells of a new day dawning. Like his father, he enjoyed a freshly roasted cup of coffee, and as he stood in the kitchen pouring himself a cup of espresso, he looked out at the vineyard and smiled. This was his haven, his joy, and each day he looked forward to tending to the vines, checking his fermentation tanks, or working in the laboratory meticulously checking his new vintages.

He reached up and opened the kitchen cupboards. He found a soup bowl and leaned over to pull the storage container on the kitchen counter closer to him. As he dished himself some of Ana's homemade muesli, he smiled to himself, arguing in his mind who made the best version. He loved the way Ana spent time with his mother Genevieve and how they shared a passion for cooking. Genevieve adored spending time with her daughter-in-law, where they often found themselves in the kitchen sharing recipes. Genevieve and Ana chatted lovingly, often sharing their best-kept secrets in the kitchen, and Genevieve was always enthusiastic to show Ana all her best-loved dishes. Jean-Pierre could visually see them in his mind now, remembering the day Genevieve showed Ana the way she laid out all the grains, nuts, and dried fruit on a flat baking tray, drizzled honey all over the mix, and placed the tray of goodness into the oven to roast. It was always a family favourite, and Genevieve was only too happy to share her recipe with Ana. Jean-Pierre loved Ana's version as she added her own twist to it, and though the ingredients were practically the same, her muesli tasted slightly different.

Jean-Pierre's mind returned to the vineyards as he spooned another mouthful of muesli into his mouth. He looked out at the rows of vines and tried to gather his thoughts on tasks he needed to do today. Oddly though, he couldn't focus, and his mind strayed to family. Again, he wondered whether his grandfather stood at the kitchen window with the same thoughts. He wondered if grandma made muesli and loved to cook, and he wondered if they too grew up in the vineyards and learnt the skills from their parents.

Jean-Pierre took his last sip of coffee and tidied up in the kitchen. He walked out into the crisp morning air and made his way to the cellar.

* * *

As Jean-Pierre walked past the corner of the building, the familiar crunch of gravel beneath his boots brought a rhythmic calm. Yet today was different. His steps faltered as his gaze was drawn to the stone wall at the edge of the château. Something about its aged texture and the way the light hit the weathered stones stopped him in his tracks.

He turned slowly, facing the grandeur of Château Dupont. For a moment, he simply stood there, his eyes tracing the silhouette of the building against the distant, snow-dusted Alps. The soft morning light bathed the château in a golden hue, accentuating its centuries-old architecture. Jean-Pierre tilted his head, his eyes moving deliberately from one window to the next, as though trying to see through the thick glass into the lives of those who had once called this place home.

"Who built this place?" he murmured aloud, the question hanging in the crisp air. "How many Duponts have walked these grounds? Did they stand where I'm standing now, wondering about the same things?"

His gaze dropped to the stone foundation at the base of the château. The walls seemed to whisper secrets; stories of eras long past. "Was it always a vineyard?" he wondered. "Or did someone dream of this—of the rows of vines, the cellars, and the bottles of wine that bear our name?"

Jean-Pierre's curiosity deepened. He felt a sudden, pressing need to know more, to uncover the roots of the family legacy that had shaped his life. "What lives have these walls witnessed? What secrets do they hold?"

He spoke to the château as if it might answer him. "How did it survive the wars, the harsh winters, and the changing times? Who were the Duponts who lived here before us? Were they anything like me?"

Jean-Pierre chuckled softly, shaking his head. "I must be losing it," he muttered, running a hand through his dark hair. But the questions kept coming, and with them, an unexpected excitement began to stir in him.

He made a mental note, firm and deliberate. *I'll ask my parents at dinner tonight. Father will know something—he always does. And if not him, then Mother. She might have stories from her side of the family too.*

He glanced at the kitchen window, half-expecting to see Genevieve inside, bustling about. A memory surfaced: his father sitting at the table, recounting tales of his own childhood, of playing among the vines and learning the art of winemaking from his father before him. Had his grandfather done the same? Had they passed down not just skills, but memories, hopes, and dreams, etched into the very stones of the château?

Jean-Pierre sighed, his breath visible in the cool air. He turned back to the path, heading for the cellar, but his mind was far from the tasks awaiting him. Instead, it was alive with questions, possibilities, and a growing desire to uncover the untold stories of the Dupont legacy.

* * *

Jean-Pierre walked around to the front gardens, the gravel path crunching softly beneath his boots. As he approached the neatly trimmed hedges and blooming flower beds, the familiar sight of his father, Marcel, greeted him from the château's balcony. Marcel stood with his espresso cup in hand, his gaze sweeping across the vineyards that stretched to the horizon.

"Morning, Jean-Pierre!" Marcel called out, his deep voice resonating in the stillness of the morning.

"Morning, *Papa*," Jean-Pierre replied, shading his eyes with his hand as he looked up at his father.

Marcel took a sip of his coffee, his eyes glinting with curiosity. "What's on the agenda for today, son?"

Jean-Pierre smiled and leaned casually against a garden post. "Oh, the usual—checking on the fermentation tanks for the latest vintage, trimming some unruly vines, and a few odd jobs that can't wait. Plenty to keep me busy."

Marcel nodded approvingly. "Good, good. Your grandfather always said, 'Every vine is a promise. A promise of hard work, care, and patience. And if we honour that promise, the vineyard will reward us.'"

Jean-Pierre chuckled, shaking his head. "Yes, *Papa*, you've drilled that into me more times than I can count. I think it's tattooed on my brain by now."

Marcel laughed a warm and familiar sound that echoed across the courtyard. But as the laughter faded, Jean-Pierre hesitated, his gaze lingering on his father. The morning sunlight highlighted the lines of Marcel's face, etched there by years of hard work and dedication.

"*Papa*," Jean-Pierre began, his voice softer now. "Did *Papi* also stand there in the mornings with his coffee? Did he look out at the vineyard like you do?"

Marcel's expression shifted, a mixture of nostalgia and pride washing over his features. He rested a hand on the balcony rail and looked out across the vines as if searching for an answer within their rows.
"Yes, he did," Marcel said finally, his voice tinged with fondness. "Your grandfather loved this land. He used to stand right here, every morning, with his coffee in hand. He'd say the same thing to me that I've said to you today. And I imagine his father before him did something similar, though I never had the chance to ask him."

Jean-Pierre smiled, a sense of connection to his family's legacy warming him from the inside. "It's like a tradition, isn't it? A Dupont rite of passage—coffee, the balcony, and a promise to the vineyard."

Marcel chuckled. "You could say that. It's more than a tradition, though. It's a way of life. These vines, this land—it's part of us. Just as we are part of it."

Jean-Pierre looked out at the vineyard, the rows of vines seeming to ripple in the soft morning breeze. "It makes me wonder how far back it all goes. How many generations of Duponts stood here, looking out at this same view, feeling the same connection."

Marcel's eyes twinkled. "That, my boy, is something worth exploring. You've always been curious, just like your mother. Perhaps it's time you started asking more questions."

Jean-Pierre nodded thoughtfully, the wheels in his mind turning. "I think I will. Maybe tonight at dinner."

Marcel raised his espresso cup in a small salute. "Good. Now get to work, or those promises out there might not keep themselves."

Jean-Pierre laughed and waved as he turned towards the vineyard, his thoughts alive with questions and possibilities, the legacy of Château Dupont pulsing through his veins.

* * *

Jean-Pierre bent over the low rows of vines, carefully pruning with the skill and precision honed over years of tending the vineyard. The midday sun was warm but pleasant, and the rhythmic snip of the pruning shears felt almost meditative. In the distance, he could hear the gentle hum of bees in the herb garden, where his mother, Genevieve, was busy tending to her plants.

"Jean-Pierre!" her voice rang out, warm and melodious, carried by the soft breeze. He straightened and turned towards her. Genevieve stood in her herb garden, a basket of freshly cut thyme and rosemary in her hands. "Don't forget dinner tonight!"

Jean-Pierre smiled, wiping the sweat from his brow with the back of his hand. "Hello, *Maman*! How could I ever forget food from the best chef in the world?"

Genevieve chuckled, a light blush colouring her cheeks. She always felt a swell of pride whenever her cooking was praised, especially by her son. Family dinners were her favourite time of the week, a tradition she cherished deeply. Friday nights at the château had become sacred, a time for everyone to gather, share stories, and enjoy a lovingly prepared meal.

Genevieve glanced towards him as he walked closer, leaning casually against the garden's low stone wall. "I'm touched, you know," she said, her voice soft. "It means so much to me that we all come together like this. Your father and I look forward to it all week."

Jean-Pierre smiled, the corners of his hazel eyes crinkling. "It's the highlight of my week too, *Maman*. You and *Papa* make this place feel like home, not just a house. I can't imagine Giselle and Pascal growing up anywhere else."

Genevieve's face lit up at the mention of her grandchildren. "They remind me so much of you and Chantelle when you were young. Always running, laughing, exploring. They have such a joy for life— it's infectious."

Jean-Pierre paused, his gaze shifting towards the herb garden. "*Maman*," he began thoughtfully, "did Mamie have a garden like this? Did she love to cook the way you do?"

Genevieve's expression softened, and she set down her basket. She brushed her hands together, shaking off remnants of soil, as memories of her late in-laws came flooding back.
"Oh, yes," she said, her voice tinged with nostalgia. "Grandma loved her garden. It wasn't as tidy as this one, but it was bursting with life. She had rows of beans, carrots, potatoes, and herbs of every kind. She'd spend hours out there, rain or shine. And her cooking—oh, Jean-Pierre, it was something special. Good, wholesome country food, the kind that sticks to your bones.

"*Papi* would hunt in the mountains, bringing home pheasant, rabbit, or sometimes venison, and Mamie would roast it with vegetables from her garden. I still remember the aromas when I first came here as a student. Your father would bring me home from university, and they'd welcome me with a feast. Everything on the table was something they had grown or gathered themselves. They were hard-working country people, living off the land. And Mamie—she made it all feel so magical, so abundant."

Jean-Pierre listened, captivated. He imagined his grandparents, *Papi* trudging back from the mountains with his game, Mamie preparing a hearty stew with her garden's bounty. The image felt vivid and grounding, connecting him to the generations that came before.

"Do you think those recipes were passed down?" he asked.

Genevieve smiled and tilted her head in thought. "Perhaps. Some of the techniques and flavours are in my cooking, too. You know what? Maybe tonight, I'll make you one of Mamie's country stews. Something hearty and nostalgic. Would you like that?"

Jean-Pierre's grin widened. "I'd love that, *Maman*. It feels like a little piece of history brought to life."

Genevieve picked up her basket and walked back towards the kitchen, glancing back at her son with a proud, affectionate smile. Jean-Pierre returned to his vines, feeling a warmth in his chest. The thought of sharing Mamie's stew with the family that evening filled him with a sense of continuity, as though the threads of their shared legacy were being woven tighter with each passing day.

* * *

The dining room at Château Dupont was alive with laughter and chatter, the warmth of the family filling every corner of the grand space. Giselle and Pascal were the first to burst through the doors, their excited voices ringing out as they ran towards their grandparents.

"Mamie! *Papi*!" they squealed in unison, throwing themselves into Genevieve's and Marcel's waiting arms. Marcel scooped up Pascal while Genevieve embraced Giselle, both grandparents beaming with joy.

Jean-Pierre and Ana entered shortly after, Jean-Pierre proudly holding up a bottle of wine. "It's still young," he announced, "but this was my vintage I worked so hard on right after your trip to Chornobyl five years ago."

Marcel's eyes lit up, and he nodded approvingly. "Ah, good! I've been looking forward to tasting this one."

For a fleeting moment, the mention of Chornobyl caused a cold shiver to run down Genevieve's spine. She paused for a second, but then quickly brushed it off, not wanting to spoil the moment. She turned to her family, focusing on the cheerful atmosphere.

"And what have you two naughty little munchkins been up to?" asked Genevieve.

"We're not naughty, Mamie?" chirped Giselle, followed by Pascal giggling and shrugging his shoulders.

No sooner had they exchanged greetings than Chantelle and Adrien arrived, Adrien holding up a bottle with a wide grin. "I asked for the best Pinot Noir at the bottle shop, and guess what they gave me? Château Dupont!" he said with mock surprise. "I wonder if you've heard of it?"

Everyone chuckled at his joke, but their attention was quickly drawn to Giselle and Pascal, who ran up to Aunty Chantelle, shouting, "Tata Chantelle!" She bent down and wrapped them both in her arms, laughing as they spoke over each other in their excitement.

Giselle piped up, "Tata Chantelle, Daddy says he can beat you at skiing!"

Chantelle shook her head with mock indignation. "Your daddy only wins when he cheats," she teased, shooting a playful glance at Jean-Pierre.

Adrien chimed in, grinning. "Maybe we should all go skiing together, Jean-Pierre, and you can prove it once and for all. But you better be careful, because I might just be faster."

The whole family laughed, joining in the banter. Marcel leaned back in his chair, his eyes twinkling. "I can't wait for winter. A family trip to the mountains sounds perfect. Nothing like a day on the slopes followed by a good fondue."

As the conversation shifted to winter plans, Genevieve began serving up steaming bowls of her country stew. "This," she said with a smile, "was one of Jean-Pierre's and Chantelle's Mamie and *Papi*'s favourite dishes. It's a little piece of history for us tonight."

She leaned towards Pascal, her voice soft and warm. "Your great-grandfather was a skilled hunter. He would bring home game from the mountains, and Mamie would cook the most wonderful meals with what they grew in the garden."

Pascal's eyes grew wide with fascination. "What did he shoot, Mamie?"

Marcel took over, his deep voice weaving a picture of country life. "*Papi* hunted rabbits, pheasants, and sometimes even wild boar. In the mountains, he'd track deer for venison. It was hard work, but that's how they lived—off the land, with great respect for nature."

As the family ate, Jean-Pierre's thoughtful expression didn't go unnoticed. After a moment of silence, he cleared his throat. "*Papa, Maman*," he began, "do we know much about our family history? When was the château built? Has it always been a winery? How far back can we trace our lineage?"

Chantelle, ever quick-witted, raised an eyebrow. "You seem keen on our history all of a sudden," she teased.

Jean-Pierre chuckled, leaning back in his chair. "I've always been curious, but lately... I don't know. It feels more important somehow. Like there's so much to learn about who we are and where we come from."

Chantelle smirked. "Maybe you should go to the archives, big brother."

Jean-Pierre nodded thoughtfully. "Maybe I will."

The conversation turned lively again as Genevieve stood, clapping her hands to grab everyone's attention. "Now," she announced, "who wants pudding?"

Giselle and Pascal shouted at the same time, "Me, me!" Giselle shot her hand into the air enthusiastically, and Pascal quickly copied her, giggling as he did.

The family burst into laughter again, the warmth and love that bound them together filling the room. For Jean-Pierre, it was another moment of clarity—a reminder of why their legacy mattered so much and why he felt driven to uncover the stories that had brought them to this point.

Chapter 3

The November morning was brisk, with a crisp chill that Jean-Pierre found invigorating. He stood at the edge of the vineyard, surveying the rows of vines that stretched like ribbons across the sloping land. The golden-brown leaves, remnants of autumn's palette, clung stubbornly to the vines, whispering in the breeze. Jean-Pierre took a deep breath, savouring the earthy scent of the soil mingled with the faint sweetness of the grapes lingering from the harvest.

The vineyard was a hive of activity. Jean-Pierre moved with practised efficiency, pruning shears in hand, meticulously removing the old wood to prepare the vines for their winter dormancy. He paused occasionally, running his fingers along the vine canes, assessing their health. "Every vine is a promise," his grandfather used to say, and Jean-Pierre worked with that mantra etched in his mind.

As he worked, his thoughts wandered to the generations before him. Had his great-grandfather walked these same rows with pruning shears in hand, stooping to tend the vines with the same care? What tools had they used, and how much of their labour had been done by hand before the advent of modern machinery? He smiled at the thought of *grand-père* and *arrière grand-père,* his grandfather and great-grandfather standing on this very land, likely muttering about the weather or the soil quality.

The day unfolded with a rhythm Jean-Pierre found deeply satisfying. After pruning, he moved to cleaning and repairing trellises. The old wooden stakes and wires bore the marks of time and needed regular attention to ensure they could support next year's growth. Later, he walked to the fermentation tanks, where the last of the year's vintages were ageing. He methodically checked the temperature and cleanliness of the tanks, his meticulous nature shining through. With November drawing to a close, preparations for December's tasks were already underway. Cover crops were sown between the rows to enrich the soil, and Jean-Pierre planned to mulch the vineyard before the first snow. There was also bottling to oversee and labelling to finalise for the wines destined for Christmas orders.

December arrived with a festive air. The Dupont family began preparations for the holiday season, and the château buzzed with activity. Genevieve and Ana spent hours in the kitchen, filling the air with the warm, inviting aromas of baking and simmering stews. Pascal and Giselle, bundled in scarves and coats, ran through the rows of vines, their laughter echoing in the crisp air.

By Christmas Eve, the château was adorned with garlands and twinkling lights. A majestic Christmas tree stood in the great hall, its branches heavy with ornaments, some passed down through generations.

The family gathered that evening for *Le Réveillon*, the traditional Christmas Eve feast. The table was laden with a feast that reflected both Swiss-French heritage and family tradition. Genevieve had prepared a rich foie gras terrine, Ana contributed a classic Swiss fondue, and there were platters of roasted meats, oysters, and savoury tarts. A steaming pot of *vin chaud* perfumed with cinnamon and orange warmed the atmosphere.

After the main course, Genevieve brought out the *pièce de résistance*: *La Bûche de Noël*, a Yule log cake adorned with meringue mushrooms and chocolate shavings. Giselle and Pascal's eyes lit up as they eagerly asked for seconds, then thirds, their enthusiasm bringing laughter to the table.

As the meal wound down, the family moved to the tree to exchange gifts. The children tore through their presents with delight, and amidst the chaos, Jean-Pierre uncorked one of the latest vintages. Marcel, Adrien, and Jean-Pierre savoured the wine, swirling it in their glasses and discussing its bouquet, strength, and lingering aromas. The vintage, born of a challenging harvest, had exceeded their expectations, and Marcel proudly declared it a testament to their family's dedication.

Chantelle approached Jean-Pierre, her hands cradling a carefully wrapped gift. "*Bon Noël*, Jean-Pierre," she said warmly, presenting it to him.

Jean-Pierre leaned forward to hug his sister, planting a kiss on each cheek. "*Merci*, Chantelle," he replied, his voice full of affection. He unwrapped the present with care, revealing an elegantly designed box. As realisation dawned, Chantelle explained, "You seemed so enthusiastic about our history, so I bought you *Family Lines*. You can trace our ancestry and family history."

Jean-Pierre's eyes lit up, and his face broke into a broad smile. Overwhelmed, he jumped to his feet, pulling Chantelle into a tighter hug and kissing her cheeks again with more fervour. "*Merci mille fois*, Chantelle," he exclaimed, his gratitude overflowing. Adrien piped up and said, "Careful Jean-Pierre, I might get jealous."

The family erupted into laughter; Chantelle included. Jean-Pierre turned to them all, holding up the gift like a prized treasure. "It is our *legacy*," he declared, his gaze sweeping over Marcel, Genevieve,

Adrien, and Chantelle, all of whom looked back at him with pride and amusement.

Chantelle grinned. "Looks like I got it right," she said, teasingly.

They all laughed, some poking fun at Jean-Pierre's exuberance, while others shared in his enthusiasm. The atmosphere was filled with warmth and cheer as the family continued their festivities, their voices mingling with the soft crackle of the fire.

The excitement settled as the clock neared midnight. The family bundled up and drove to their local church for *Messe de Minuit*, the Midnight Mass. The small stone church, illuminated by soft candlelight, was a vision of serenity. The stained-glass windows, mosaics of vibrant reds and blues, glowed faintly against the darkened sky, telling stories of saints and miracles.

Inside, the scent of incense mingled with the pine of Christmas wreaths. Neighbours and friends greeted each other warmly, their shared joy palpable. Jean-Pierre carried a drowsy Giselle, and Ana held Pascal, both children fast asleep.

The choir began a soft rendition of "*Minuit, Chrétiens*," their harmonies filling the vaulted ceiling with reverence. The priest's sermon reflected on hope, community, and the importance of family, and the flicker of candlelight added to the magical atmosphere. Jean-Pierre dwelled for a moment on the priest's words and repeated quietly to himself *The importance of family*. He smiled and couldn't wait to get into *Family Lines* and start uncovering his family tree.

After mass, they drove back to the château, and the children were gently tucked into bed, their dreams filled with Christmas magic. The adults gathered in the sitting room for a final toast. Marcel poured glasses of a fine Armagnac, and they reflected on the year.

"It's been a good vintage," Jean-Pierre said, lifting his glass.

Adrien grinned and added, "And into the new year, I look forward to skiing with you, Jean-Pierre. Let's see if you can keep up."

Laughter rang out, and as the fire crackled in the hearth, the family toasted to the promise of a new year filled with love, tradition, and the shared legacy of the vineyard.

Chapter 4

The auditorium was a sea of anticipation as Marcel Dupont concluded his lecture. Standing under the soft glow of the stage lights, he exuded calm authority, his presence commanding the attention of every dignitary, scientist, and student present. The screen behind him displayed the remnants of a simulated cosmic explosion, fiery tendrils of a supernova fading into a brilliant swirl of stars.

"Disorder, havoc and destruction," Marcel declared, his voice measured yet captivating, "are the architects of creation. From the collapse of a star, we find the seeds of galaxies. While supernovae play a critical role in enriching the interstellar medium with heavy elements, galaxy formation is a more complex process that involves gravity, dark matter, and the dynamics of baryonic matter over time. Black holes devour matter, but their gravitational pull shapes the universe. Gamma-ray bursts, though devastating, illuminate the vastness of space. These are the paradoxes of our universe: destruction begets life, and death paves the way for rebirth."

He paused, allowing the weight of his words to settle over the audience. "In every cosmic wave, every pulse of light lies a story—a testament to the universe's relentless march towards complexity and renewal."

The audience erupted into applause, their admiration felt and shown in every soul in the room. Many stood, their clapping intensifying as the Dean of the University walked onto the stage with a proud smile.

"Ladies and gentlemen," the Dean began, "Professor Marcel Dupont has once again reminded us of the awe-inspiring forces that govern our existence. Let's take a moment to appreciate his extraordinary insights." The applause swelled, echoing through the vast hall.

Once the noise subsided, the Dean gestured to the crowd. "Professor Dupont has kindly agreed to take a few questions. Please, raise your hands."

A fellow professor stood first, his tone probing but respectful. "Professor Dupont, are you suggesting that by analysing light, we can trace it back to its origin? To the exact event that generated it?"

Marcel nodded, his mind already racing. "Precisely. Light, though ephemeral, carries with it a fingerprint—a unique identifier of its source. By studying the spectrum, intensity, and direction, we can piece together the story of its birth. Whether it was forged in the heart of a star or cast into the void by a gamma-ray burst, every photon carries its heritage."

The room buzzed with murmurs of fascination. A scientist in the back rose next, his voice ringing with curiosity. "So you're saying, theoretically, we could backtrack and find what created Earth? Our solar system? Even our galaxy?"

Marcel's expression softened, and for a fleeting moment, his thoughts turned to Jean-Pierre. The image of his son meticulously pruning vines, exploring his ancestral roots, struck him. Wasn't Jean-Pierre doing on Earth what he, Marcel, sought to do in the cosmos?

"Yes," Marcel replied, his voice tinged with reverence. "In a sense, tracing light source is akin to an ancestral quest—a journey through time to uncover origins, connections, and the forces that shaped what we are today."

He paused, his gaze sweeping the room. "The cosmos, like us, has a lineage. And every discovery we make, every light we trace, is a step closer to understanding not just the universe's story but our own place within it."

The room was silent for a moment before applause erupted again, this time mingled with hushed voices of wonder. Marcel stepped back, allowing the Dean to reclaim the stage, but his mind lingered on the parallel. The thought of Jean-Pierre unravelling their family's past and his own pursuit of the universe's origins felt beautifully interconnected—a profound reminder that exploration, whether cosmic or personal, was what defined humanity's spirit.

* * *

As the sun dipped low on the horizon, casting a hazy orange glow across the road, Marcel's mind danced with thoughts of ancestors and legacies. He navigated the winding streets with a sense of purpose, the rhythm of the engine matching the cadence of his racing ideas. Jean-Pierre's enthusiasm had a way of igniting sparks of inspiration within him, and today was no different. The tumultuous applause and sense of appreciation he received from the audience at his lecture seemed to light a fire within him.

The link between their pursuits crystallised in his mind, each ancestral thread weaving a tapestry that bound them not just to the past but to a future filled with promise. Marcel chuckled softly, imagining the possibility of a grand project that could intertwine their ideas, but a cautious voice in his head reminded him of the need for moderation. He had been overly ambitious before, chasing after too many grand schemes until they unravelled like threads pulled from a well-worn garment.

Resigned but hopeful, Marcel shelved his ambitious thoughts for another day. He knew that the real magic lay in collaboration, in joining forces with someone who shared his fervour for discovery. Jean-Pierre, with his intense gaze and heartfelt connection to their shared heritage, seemed the perfect partner for an endeavour such as this. Once this was done, he could then possibly consider his idea. Arriving at his modest home, Marcel felt a rush of excitement and determination. He could almost see the two of them poring over dusty old records and family trees, drawing connections between their lineages. Resilience was the anchor they would explore together—a pillar of strength that had carried their ancestors through hardship.

Later that evening, under the soft amber glow of his desk lamp, Marcel thought of Jean-Pierre and wanted to invite him to collaborate on a systematic exploration of their family trees. He then thought he'd wait for Jean-Pierre to approach him and let him dwell in his enthusiastic research for now, having seen how keen his son was on embarking on this journey. The sky turned deep blue outside his window, stars emerging one by one, mirroring the constellation of ideas that filled his mind.

He smiled, envisioning their discussions stretching into the night, where enthusiasm would merge with tenacity, mapping out not just lineages but the very essence of who they were. With a sense of quiet anticipation, Marcel knew he had taken the first step towards something profound—a journey that held the potential to uncover not just family histories but also the very fabric of their identities. He waited patiently for now, knowing that Jean-Pierre would approach him soon, and he couldn't wait to join him in his quest.

Chapter 5

The winter chill settled over the Dupont estate, blanketing the vineyards in quiet stillness. With the bustle of November and pre-Christmas vineyard tasks behind him and now into the new year, Jean-Pierre found himself with rare pockets of time, the perfect opportunity to embark on his new project. The family lineage kit from Chantelle sat on his desk, an invitation to uncover the hidden stories of generations past.

He opened his laptop one crisp morning, the warm glow of the fireplace casting flickering shadows across the room. Logging into *Family Lines*, he began by entering the basic details of his family history—names, dates of birth, and known locations. The interface was intuitive, guiding him step by step. As he typed, a sense of anticipation surged within him. It felt like opening a treasure chest, not knowing what relics or surprises he might uncover.

The system prompted him to submit his DNA sample for deeper analysis, a process he had already begun with the kit Chantelle had gifted him. The thought of his genetic material mapping out his family tree excited him. He would then dig deeper on his own accord, researching names at local libraries. This idea of unlocking centuries of stories filled him with curiosity.

Who were the Duponts? he wondered. *Where did we come from? What trials and triumphs shaped the lives of those who came before us? I wonder how much I can dig up at the libraries and archives?*

Once his registration was complete, Jean-Pierre leaned back in his chair, a determined glint in his hazel eyes. This was only the beginning.

***

Later that week, Jean-Pierre sat at the long oak dining table with Marcel and Genevieve, a pot of coffee steaming between them. Marcel smiled to himself. He knew his son would come to him sooner or later. Papers, notebooks, and old family photographs were spread out like puzzle pieces waiting to be arranged.

"I want to be as thorough as possible," Jean-Pierre said, his voice tinged with enthusiasm. "But I need a plan, a structure to follow. Otherwise, I'll drown in all the information."

Marcel nodded, his scientific mind already shifting into problem-solving mode. "You need a template," he said, pulling a blank sheet of paper towards him. "Something systematic. Start with what you know—dates, names, locations—and work backwards."

Genevieve, ever the organised one, chimed in. "Don't forget to look for marital records, death certificates, and even property deeds. They can reveal connections that aren't immediately obvious."

Together, they drafted a guideline. Marcel's scientific precision complemented Genevieve's attention to detail, and Jean-Pierre absorbed their advice eagerly. The template included columns for names, birth and death dates, locations, occupations, and any notable anecdotes or achievements.

"Think of it like solving a jigsaw puzzle," Marcel said. "Each piece might not seem significant on its own, but when you start putting them together, the bigger picture emerges."

Jean-Pierre nodded, grateful for his parents' involvement. It was more than just a project now; it was a shared journey, a way to honour their heritage together.

***

Jean-Pierre spent his mornings at the local library, where the scent of aged books and the quiet hum of activity created a tranquil atmosphere. He dove into public records, meticulously searching through birth and death registries, marriage licenses, and census data. Every discovery, no matter how small, felt like a victory.

One day, while leafing through an old ledger, he stumbled upon a record for Pierre Dupont, a winemaker in the late 1800s who had lived not far from their current estate. The coincidence thrilled him. *Could this Pierre be an ancestor?* he wondered, jotting down the details to investigate further.

Jean-Pierre's afternoons were spent in the château's library, where he pored over family heirlooms and documents. Marcel often joined him, the two of them losing track of time as they discussed possible connections and speculated about the lives of their ancestors.

"You know," Marcel said one evening, holding an old photograph of a stern-looking man in a suit. "I wonder if he ever imagined his descendants would be sitting here, trying to piece together his story." Jean-Pierre smiled. "It makes me feel connected to something bigger," he said. "Like we're not just individuals but part of a continuous thread."

***

As the days turned into weeks, Jean-Pierre began to see patterns emerging. He created a digital family tree, filling in names and dates as he uncovered them. Each addition felt like placing another brick in a foundation, solidifying their family's history.

Genevieve contributed by recounting stories she had heard from her parents, grandparents, and in-laws, tales of perseverance and hardship that brought the names on the tree to life. "Your great-grandmother, Marie," she said one evening, "used to make the most incredible *tarte Tatin*. She believed cooking was a way of preserving love across generations."

Jean-Pierre made a note to include these anecdotes in his records. It wasn't just about dates and locations but also the essence of the people who had come before them. He realised too that it wasn't just about his paternal lineage but also loved hearing from his mother about his maternal side.

***

Winter settled firmly over the estate, and the winery's operations slowed to a quiet hum. Jean-Pierre relished the stillness, using the time to delve deeper into his research. He sent enquiries to local archives and genealogical societies, each reply bringing new fragments of information.

One snowy afternoon, while reviewing his findings with Marcel, a realisation struck him. "You know," he said, "this isn't just our family's story. It's also a piece of history—how people lived, what they valued, how they survived."

Marcel nodded thoughtfully. "It's humbling, isn't it? To see how our existence is built on the efforts and sacrifices of those who came before us."

Jean-Pierre smiled. "It's our legacy," he said softly, echoing the words he had spoken on Christmas Eve.

***

The project became a family affair, with everyone contributing in their own way. Chantelle provided medical insights into genetic patterns, while Adrien offered his tech-savvy skills to help digitise records. Ana, with her calm demeanour and attention to detail, proofread documents and helped organise the growing collection of data.

On evenings when the family gathered by the fire, Jean-Pierre would share his latest discoveries, sparking lively discussions and deepening their collective appreciation for their roots.

As winter's grip tightened, Jean-Pierre looked at the growing family tree with a sense of accomplishment. There was still much to uncover, but the foundation had been laid. And in the process, he had not only learned about his ancestors but also strengthened the bonds with his family, creating new memories to pass down to future generations.

The Dupont legacy, it seemed, was as much about the present as it was about the past.

Mario Zatta

Chapter 6

The scent of roasting meat filled the air as Jean-Pierre pushed open the heavy oak door of the château. The warmth of the kitchen embraced him, a sharp contrast to the crisp winter air outside. Laughter and conversation drifted towards him; the familiar rhythm of his family gathered for their traditional Friday night dinner.

He set down his leather satchel on the side table, shrugging off his coat and scarf. As he entered the kitchen, Giselle and Pascal darted towards him, their little feet pattering against the tiled floor.

"*Papa*!" Giselle exclaimed, throwing her arms around his legs. Pascal followed, his bright eyes wide with excitement.
Jean-Pierre bent down, scooping them both up effortlessly. He kissed Giselle on her cheek, then Pascal, who giggled as he squirmed in his father's arms.

"I wondered where you were," Genevieve called from the oven, her voice filled with warmth. She was basting the roast, her sleeves rolled up, while Ana stood beside her, carefully checking the potatoes.

Jean-Pierre set the children down and crossed the room to plant a kiss on his mother's cheek. "*Ma Maman*," he greeted softly, his voice full of affection.

Ana straightened from the oven, holding a steaming tray with oven gloves. Jean-Pierre leaned in to kiss her on the lips. "*Ma Chérie*," he said, the tenderness in his voice making her smile.

"We were waiting for you, Jean-Pierre," Adrien teased from the dining room, where he was helping Marcel lay the table. "We need some wine, and I'm thirsty!"

Everyone laughed, including Marcel, who glanced up from placing the silverware. "Yes, Jean-Pierre. I'm counting on you to make an excellent selection tonight," he said with a mock seriousness.

Jean-Pierre grinned, ruffling Pascal's hair as he made his way to the antique oak wine cabinet that stood proudly between the kitchen and dining room. It was a piece of craftsmanship, aged yet elegant, its carved doors polished to a soft sheen. Jean-Pierre opened it, his fingers tracing the labels as he scanned the collection. He chose a vintage he knew everyone would enjoy and returned to the kitchen, bottle in hand.

"I may have some exciting news for you all," he announced as he uncorked the wine.

Marcel raised an eyebrow, intrigued. "Oh? What have you found?"

Jean-Pierre poured the wine, his face lighting up with excitement. "I've uncovered records of our *arrière-grand-pères*, great grandfathers five generations back to Henri Dupont. It seems the château was built in 1650 during the reconstruction of Europe after the Thirty Years' War and Henri it seems started the vineyard back then."

The room fell silent for a moment, then erupted in voices all at once. "Did great-granddad build the château, *Papa*?" Giselle asked, tugging on his sleeve.

Pascal's eyes widened as he sat at the table, looking at Jean-Pierre with silent anticipation.

Ana clapped her hands together. "That's incredible! Can you imagine? The vision he must have had to create something like this at such a time."

Jean-Pierre raised his hand slightly, signalling for quiet, and leaned forward with a proud smile. "It's a fascinating story, and one I think we all should know. Let me tell you about the generations of Duponts who have shaped our family legacy."

"It all began with Henri Dupont, born in the early 1600s, around the time of the Thirty Years' War. Europe was in turmoil, but Henri saw an opportunity amidst the turmoil. In 1650, he built this château and planted the first vines that started our vineyard. He was a man of resilience and vision, determined to create something lasting even during one of the most challenging periods in European history." Jean-Pierre's voice took on a storytelling cadence as the family leaned in.

"Henri's work laid the foundation, but it was Étienne Dupont, born in the late 1600s, who brought innovation. During the Enlightenment, he introduced scientific techniques to winemaking, experimenting and elevating the vineyard's reputation. Étienne believed in progress and rationality, ensuring that the estate thrived during an era of intellectual and cultural change.

"Then there was Jean-Baptiste Dupont, born around the 1760s. He guided the family estate through the turbulence of the French Revolution. While supporting the ideals of liberty and equality, Jean-Baptiste managed to protect the château and the vineyards. His ability to adapt and survive during such a volatile time is the reason our family legacy endured."

He paused for a moment, taking a sip of wine.

"Fast forward to the 19th century, and we have Charles Dupont, born in the 1860s. Charles rebuilt parts of the château, blending its traditional architecture with modern advancements of the time. He also modernised the vineyard, preparing it for the challenges of the 20th century. He was a true visionary, embracing industrial progress while holding on to our heritage."

Jean-Pierre's expression softened as he continued. "And then there's Louis Dupont, born at the dawn of the 20th century, my grandfather. Louis not only renovated the château in the mid-1900s but also lived through and survived World War II. This very château survived the war. He passed on to my father, Marcel, a deep respect for resilience, history, and intellectual curiosity."

Marcel, sitting quietly at the head of the table, gave a subtle nod, his eyes glistening with emotion.

"And finally, we have my father, Marcel," Jean-Pierre said with pride. "Born in the 1950s, he carries forward the values of fortitude, innovation and knowledge. As a physicist and steward of the vineyard, he's woven together science and tradition, proving that our legacy isn't just about preserving the past—it's about shaping the future."

Jean-Pierre's gaze shifted to his children, his voice softening. "And now, Pascal and Giselle, it's your turn to carry this story forward. Our family's strength and perseverance run through your veins. You are part of something extraordinary—a lineage that has survived wars, revolutions, and countless challenges to stand strong today."

The room fell silent again, but this time with a sense of reverence. Ana reached over and took Jean-Pierre's hand. "What a story," she said softly.

Pascal looked up at his sister, then back at his father with wide eyes. "Do you think I can be like Henri or Louis when I grow up?"

Jean-Pierre chuckled, leaning down to tousle Pascal's hair. "Of course you can, Pascal. Just keep helping us take care of the vines and learning the stories. One day, you'll be a big part of it too."

Adrien leaned back against the counter, crossing his arms. "It makes you wonder about the strength of character it took to rebuild after the war. Maybe I should look into my own family's history. Who knows what I might find?"

Jean-Pierre smirked. "Maybe Chantelle should look into your family history before she marries you," he teased.

Chantelle blushed furiously, giving Jean-Pierre a sharp look. "Oh, very funny," she said, her tone dry.

Genevieve chimed in, shaking her head. "Jean-Pierre, behave yourself."

Ana gave him a playful nudge. "Honestly, you'll never grow up."

Marcel cleared his throat, his expression thoughtful. "I would be very interested to find out more about *arrière-grandpère* Charles. There must be war records, perhaps even stories about his role in the rebuilding efforts."

The conversation shifted to World War I as Marcel continued. "It was a devastating time for France. Entire villages were wiped out, the land was scarred, and so many lives were lost."

Jean-Pierre poured wine for everyone, and the family settled into their seats, listening as Marcel described the war period.

***

Marcel leaned forward, his glass of wine in hand. "The First World War, or *La Grande Guerre*, as it was known here, was brutal. France was one of the major battlegrounds. The trenches stretched across the country, from the Vosges Mountains to the North Sea. Millions of soldiers fought in those trenches, enduring the cold, the mud, and the constant threat of attack."

Chantelle nodded, her expression sombre. "I can't imagine the horror they lived through. And the destruction…"

Marcel gestured with his glass. "Entire regions were reduced to rubble. Villages like ours were left in ruins. But after the war, the French people showed remarkable resilience. They rebuilt not just their homes, but their lives, their farms, and their industries."

Adrien spoke up. "And the vineyard would have been part of that, right? If Charles renovated it then, he must have been rebuilding from troubled times and with nothing."

Marcel nodded. "Exactly. The war ended in 1918, but the aftermath lingered for years. Fields had to be cleared of debris and unexploded shells. People had to replant crops and rebuild homes. It was an era of immense hardship, but also determination."

Ana leaned forward. "Do you think Charles' decision to modernise the vineyard, and its practices was part of that resilience?"

"Absolutely," Marcel said. "Upgrading or restarting a vineyard after such devastation would have been a statement—a way of saying, 'We will endure.'"

Giselle, who had been listening intently, piped up. "*Papa*, did great-granddad fight in the war?"

Jean-Pierre shook his head. "I don't know yet, sweetheart. But I'll find out."

Marcel leaned back, his gaze thoughtful. "And yet again, from disorder comes rebirth," he said, his voice filled with quiet reverence.

The family sat in reflective silence for a moment, the weight of history settling over them. Then, slowly, the conversation turned back to lighter topics, but the story of Henri and Charles Dupont stayed with them, a testament to the fortitude that defined their family.

Mario Zatta

Chapter 7

The polished mahogany desk gleamed under the dim light of the mayor's study. Robert Garnier leaned back in his chair, fingers entwined, his expression unreadable. He had spent decades carefully constructing his career—cultivating allies, eliminating obstacles, and ensuring that certain historical narratives remained undisputed. The Dupont name was nothing more than a footnote in the region's long history, and that was how it should stay. Yet now, Jean-Pierre Dupont was stirring the past. His enquiries into the château's history had reached ears they shouldn't have. Garnier had ignored it at first—just a curious vintner playing historian. But then, whispers surfaced about records being pulled, questions being asked, and interest in certain wartime events that were best left buried. Garnier knew well enough that the past was never as silent as people hoped. And silence, in his world, was invaluable.

Across the desk, Gaspard and Leo, his most trusted enforcers, sat in patient stillness. Gaspard, burly and imposing, cracked his knuckles absently. Leo, wiry and sharp-eyed, leaned forward, sensing their employer's intent.

"I need you to keep an eye on this Dupont fellow," Garnier said, his voice smooth but firm. "He's stirring up things that should remain undisturbed."

Gaspard exchanged a glance with Leo before nodding. "Subtle?" he asked.

Garnier sighed, swirling the brandy in his glass. "For now. A few well-placed reminders that not all doors should be opened. No need for anything... overt." He met their gazes. "Unless he doesn't take the hint."

Leo smirked. "Consider it done."

***

Jean-Pierre was oblivious to the storm gathering around him. He spent the morning poring over records in his office, cross-referencing dates and names, trying to piece together a clearer picture of the château's past. Something about the mid-twentieth century remained frustratingly opaque. Old deeds and land transfers were missing, and wartime accounts conflicted with official records. He had told Chantelle and Adrien over breakfast that he planned to visit the municipal archives soon. Perhaps a librarian or archivist might shed light on the missing gaps.

By late afternoon, he decided to take a break. He and Adrien walked into town, aiming to pick up supplies and clear their minds. The narrow streets of the village bustled with local merchants and visitors, the air rich with the scent of fresh bread and roasting chestnuts. The casual hum of conversation and the occasional ringing of a bicycle bell gave the town its usual idyllic charm.

But something felt... off.

At first, it was barely noticeable—a lingering glance, a shadow shifting just out of view. A figure leaning against a lamppost too long, another casually adjusting his hat at the café across the street. As Jean-Pierre and Adrien browsed through a bookshop, a heavyset man in a worn coat stood outside, pretending to check his phone but clearly watching them through the window.

Jean-Pierre frowned but said nothing. Maybe he was imagining things.

It wasn't until they stopped by the butcher's shop that the unease solidified. As Adrien placed their order, Jean-Pierre turned to step outside for air, only to find himself face-to-face with a man he didn't recognise.

Tall, with a lean frame and an unsettling grin, the stranger tipped his hat. "Monsieur Dupont," he said, voice low and even. "A word of advice, if I may?"

Jean-Pierre stiffened. "Do I know you?"

The man ignored the question. "Some things are better left in the past. Dig too deep, and you might not like what you find."

Jean-Pierre narrowed his eyes. "Is that a threat?"

The man chuckled. "A friendly warning." He adjusted his cuff, revealing a faint tattoo on his wrist—a symbol Jean-Pierre couldn't quite place. Then, just as quickly as he appeared, the man turned on his heel and disappeared into the crowd.

Adrien rejoined him moments later, oblivious to what had just transpired. "Everything alright?"

Jean-Pierre hesitated, scanning the street, but the man was gone. He exhaled slowly. "Yeah," he murmured, slipping his hands into his pockets. "Let's head back."

As they walked, his mind raced. Someone was watching him. Someone who didn't want the past uncovered.

The question was—why?

Mario Zatta

Chapter 8

The sun shone brightly over the Alps, its light glinting off the pristine snow as the Dupont family hit the slopes for a day of skiing. Jean-Pierre stood at the top of a steep run, his skis crunching on the powdery surface. Adrien leaned on his poles next to him, grinning.

"Ready, Jean-Pierre?" Adrien challenged; his tone playful but competitive.

Jean-Pierre smirked. "Always."

From behind them, Chantelle chimed in, adjusting her helmet. "Don't forget, boys—you've got to beat me first."

Adrien chuckled. "We'll see about that."

Meanwhile, at the base of the slopes, Ana was tending to the children. Giselle was taking her first ski lessons, her tiny skis wobbling as she followed the instructor's guidance. Pascal, too young to ski just yet, was busy building an elaborate snowman with Ana's help. She glanced up the mountain, catching sight of Jean-Pierre's figure disappearing over the ridge.

Jean-Pierre, after completing a swift run down the slope, skied over to check on Ana and the kids. "How's it going here?" he asked, planting his poles in the snow.

"Giselle's a natural," Ana said proudly, waving towards their daughter, who was carefully sliding down a gentle slope under the instructor's watchful eye.

"And Pascal?" Jean-Pierre asked, ruffling his son's hat-covered head. "We're on our third snowman," Ana laughed.

Satisfied, Jean-Pierre kissed Ana lightly on the cheek. "I'll be back after another run. Keep an eye on Adrien—he thinks he can beat me," he joked before pushing off again.

***

Farther up the mountain, Genevieve and Marcel skied calmly down the slope like seasoned pros. Genevieve's movements were fluid and graceful, her skis carving elegant arcs in the snow. She glanced ahead to see Chantelle and Adrien skiing side by side, laughing and joking as they descended.

A warm smile spread across Genevieve's face. She was reminded of the early days of her relationship with Marcel, when they had spent countless winters skiing together, revelling in the beauty of the mountains and the thrill of the snow.

"They remind me of us," she called out to Marcel, her voice carrying over the sound of skis slicing through the snow.

Marcel, slightly behind her, caught up and looked ahead at Chantelle and Adrien. His expression softened. "They do," he agreed.

Genevieve thought about how Adrien brought out the best in Chantelle. She was smiling more, her usual reserved demeanour lightened by Adrien's exuberance.

"He's good for her," Genevieve said aloud, almost to herself. "They make a good team—like you and me."

Marcel nodded, his thoughts echoing hers. Chantelle had grown into a remarkable young woman—intelligent, driven, and compassionate. Adrien's gentle, adventurous spirit seemed to complement her perfectly.

***

At the next ski lift, Jean-Pierre caught up with the group. Adrien pointed at him with his ski pole. "Ready for round two, Jean-Pierre?" Chantelle grinned mischievously. "Let's see if you can keep up this time."

The three of them hopped off the ski lift and launched down the slope together. Jean-Pierre leaned into his skis, determined to gain the lead, but Chantelle cut past him with precision, her edges carving the snow expertly. Adrien, not to be outdone, took a more daring approach, flying straight down the steepest part of the slope.

The three skiers raced neck and neck towards the bottom, their laughter echoing in the crisp air. At the finish line, they slid to a stop, nearly in unison, and burst out laughing.

"That was a good run!" Adrien exclaimed, holding up his hand for high-fives.

Chantelle and Jean-Pierre slapped his hand, grinning.

***

The family regrouped and decided it was time for lunch. Picking up Ana and the kids, they rode the chairlift to a cosy mountain restaurant halfway up the slope. The wooden chalet was warm and inviting, with a roaring fire and the smell of hearty Alpine cuisine wafting through the air.

They sat at a long wooden table, their cheeks flushed from the cold. The adults ordered steaming bowls of fondue, crispy schnitzel, and buttery rösti, while the children were treated to hot chocolate and shared a plate of schnitzel with fries. Adrien ordered a round of schnapps for the adults, raising his glass in a toast.

"To family," he said, his voice filled with sincerity.

"To family," they echoed, clinking glasses.

The meal was lively, filled with stories, laughter, and the occasional burst of giggles from the kids. Marcel and Genevieve looked on, their hearts full as they watched their family together.

***

After lunch, Marcel, Genevieve, Ana, and the kids descended to the lower slopes, while Jean-Pierre, Chantelle, and Adrien decided to tackle the highest run.

At the summit, Jean-Pierre paused to adjust his goggles and noticed a small memorial off to the side. Intrigued, he skied over to take a closer look. The plaque, partially covered in snow, commemorated soldiers who had fought and fallen in the surrounding region during the world wars.

The conversation from dinner the other night resurfaced in his mind. He thought of Charles Dupont, his great-grandfather, and the strength of mind and soul it must have taken to rebuild the vineyard and the château after the devastation of war. He checked the plaque to see if he could see names but couldn't make it out through his goggles.

"Jean-Pierre!" Adrien's voice called out, snapping him from his thoughts. "Come on, or we'll leave you behind!"

Jean-Pierre gave the memorial one last look before pushing off to join the others, his mind swirling with thoughts of history, family, and the legacy they were uncovering.

Chapter 9

The winter frost settled over the Dupont vineyard, the vines dormant under a blanket of snow. With the pace of work slowing to a crawl, Jean-Pierre found himself with an unusual amount of free time. Though he still walked the vineyard daily, inspecting the rows of vines with the care of a steward guarding a treasure, his mind often wandered to his burgeoning genealogy project.

The discovery of Charles Dupont, his great-grandfather, had ignited a curiosity that grew stronger each day. Who was Charles? What hardships had he faced rebuilding the vineyard after World War I? And what of the generations before him? These questions consumed Jean-Pierre, driving him to delve deeper into the family's past.

Jean-Pierre's quest took him to libraries in neighbouring towns. He began with the local archives in Lausanne, a short drive from the château. The building was old, its sandstone walls weathered by time, but inside it was a trove of records—death certificates, marriage registries, and property deeds—waiting to be uncovered.
Jean-Pierre worked methodically, sifting through boxes of faded documents and scrolling through reels of microfilm. His fingers

smudged with ink and dust, he pieced together fragments of his family's story.

One day, while poring over an index of death records from the early 20th century, he found Charles's name.

Charles Dupont *Born: 1872 Died: 1953*

The dates were just numbers on a page, but they hinted at a man who had lived through monumental events—two world wars, the Great Depression, and the rebirth of a nation. Jean-Pierre's heart raced as he followed the trail to marriage records. There, he found an entry for Charles and his wife, Elise.

Marriage Record: *Charles Dupont and Elise Moreau Married: April 14, 1895*

The date, marking a time of optimism at the close of the 19th century, painted a picture in Jean-Pierre's mind: Charles and Elise standing together in the local church, their vows exchanged as France embraced a new era of progress and industrialization. He imagined them envisioning a bright future, determined to build a legacy for their family and the vineyard.

Jean-Pierre's next step was to uncover more about Charles's role in the war and his son Louis. He turned to military archives, requesting service records and combing through databases. It took weeks, but eventually, he received a scanned copy of a service card from the Ministry of Defence.

Service Record - *Name: Charles Dupont Service role: Logistics coordinator Regiment: 151st Infantry Regiment Active Duty: 1915– 1918*

Service Record - *Name: Louis Dupont Rank: Private First Class Regiment: 151st Infantry Regiment Active Duty: 1914–1918*

The 151st Infantry Regiment had been stationed on the Western Front, enduring some of the war's fiercest battles. Jean-Pierre researched the regiment's history, reading about the Battle of Verdun and the gruelling trench warfare. He imagined Louis as a young man, barely in his twenties, trudging through the mud, dodging shells, and watching comrades fall. His father, an older man, offered his services as a logistics coordinator.

The records hinted at a commendation for bravery during a retreat— a detail that filled Jean-Pierre with pride. He thought about the sacrifices Louis must have made and the fortitude it took to return home, rebuild the vineyard, and start a family.

***

Jean-Pierre often took walks around the château and its surrounding villages, letting the land itself speak to him. The vineyard lay nestled in a valley, surrounded by gentle hills and dotted with small hamlets. In the distance, the snow-capped Alps stood as silent witnesses to centuries of history.

The nearby village of Saint-Clair, with its cobblestone streets and centuries-old church, seemed frozen in time. Jean-Pierre imagined Charles and Louis walking those same streets, perhaps stopping to barter for supplies or exchanging news of the war with neighbours.

He thought about the devastation the war must have brought to this peaceful region. The fields, now lush and fertile, would have been scarred with trenches and craters. The villages, now bustling with life, would have been eerily quiet, their inhabitants either gone to fight or struggling to survive.

Jean-Pierre tried to picture the aftermath—the rebuilding, the rebirth. He thought of Charles and Elise working side by side, planting vines and tending to the land. He imagined the joy they must have felt when the first post-war harvest came in, a testament to their perseverance.

Ancestry Lines

***

As the weeks went on, Jean-Pierre's research began to form a clearer picture of the Dupont family's history. He traced the family line back through parish records, discovering Charles's parents, Jean-Baptiste and Marguerite Dupont.

Jean-Baptiste had been a farmer, growing wheat and tending livestock on land that would eventually extend and become part of a greater vineyard. Marguerite, according to baptismal records, was the daughter of a schoolteacher—a detail that intrigued Jean-Pierre. Perhaps the emphasis on education and innovation in the family had started with her.

But it was Charles and Louis who seemed to embody the family's courage and tenacity. Jean-Pierre uncovered more details about their post-war efforts to rebuild. A property deed from 1921 showed Charles purchasing additional land, expanding the vineyard to its current size. An old photograph, found in a local historical society, showed Charles and his son Louis standing proudly among the vines, his face weathered but determined.

One day, while scanning microfilm at the library in Geneva, Jean-Pierre stumbled upon a reference to a "Dupont" in a collection of wartime correspondence. The document, dated 1943, mentioned the name in connection with a group of local resistance fighters during World War II.

The reference was vague, but it sent a shiver down Jean-Pierre's spine. Could it be connected to his family? Was there more to the Duponts' story than he had imagined?

He made a note to follow up on the lead, already anticipating his next visit to the archives.

***

That evening, as Jean-Pierre sat by the fire at the château, he reflected on all he had uncovered. He thought about Charles's life, about the unimaginable hardships he must have endured and the strength it took to keep going.

Jean-Pierre looked around the room, at the stone walls that had stood through two world wars, at the vineyard beyond the windows, now dormant but alive with promise. He felt a deep connection to his ancestors, and a sense of gratitude for their courage, perseverance, and determination.

As he prepared for bed, Jean-Pierre's thoughts returned to the reference to the French Resistance. He wondered what new discoveries awaited him and what stories of courage and sacrifice might still be hidden, waiting to be uncovered.

* * *

Jean-Pierre woke early, his mind buzzing with anticipation. The promise of discovery hung in the crisp morning air as he dressed quickly, ready to dive into more research at the library. The thought of uncovering hidden details about the French Resistance sent a thrill through him. He grabbed his satchel, stuffed with notes and documents, and stepped out of his cottage not far from the château. As he made his way towards his car, a faint light flickered in the kitchen at the château. Curious, Jean-Pierre paused and peered through the window from afar. The silhouette of his father, Marcel, moved with measured precision, pouring water into the coffee maker.

Jean-Pierre smiled. "*Papa*," he called, as he walked across and stepped into the room.

Marcel turned, his expression softening when he saw his son. "Jean-Pierre? What brings you here so early?"

Before Jean-Pierre could answer, the gentle sound of slippers on the tiled floor announced Genevieve's arrival. She entered the kitchen, her robe tied snugly around her and greeted Jean-Pierre with a warm hug.

"Good morning, my darling," she said. "Coffee?"

Marcel, already ahead of her, poured a cup and placed it in front of Jean-Pierre, motioning for him to sit.

"I was just on my way to the library to look through war archives," Jean-Pierre said eagerly.

Marcel raised an eyebrow, intrigued. "Oh? What have you found so far?"

Jean-Pierre leaned forward; his voice almost conspiratorial. "*Papa*, what do you know about the French Resistance?"

At his question, both Marcel and Genevieve exchanged glances. Marcel, ever the scientist and historian at heart, took a seat and leaned back in his chair, his fingers steepled as he began to speak.

"The French Resistance," he began, "was a network of brave individuals who fought against the German occupation during World War II. They were ordinary citizens—teachers, farmers, even vintners like us—who risked everything to sabotage the enemy and protect their homeland. They used code, radio transmissions, and clandestine meetings to orchestrate their efforts."

Genevieve, listening intently, tilted her head. "Why do you ask, Jean-Pierre?"

Jean-Pierre explained his discovery—a vague reference to the name "Dupont" in a wartime document—and his belief that there might be more to uncover. Marcel, suddenly thoughtful, rubbed his chin.

"You know," he said, "now that you mention letters, there are old photograph albums and shoeboxes filled with letters in the attic. They've been there for years. Perhaps we should take a look."

Jean-Pierre followed his father up the staircase. The air was thick with the scent of aged wood and memories long forgotten. Heavy wooden beams crossed above, creaking softly under the weight of history. Jean-Pierre felt as though he had stepped into a time capsule, each room whispering secrets of its former inhabitants. The grand staircase spiralled upward, each step an echo of lives lived and struggles endured. He'd played here with Chantelle and been here numerous times before, though not in the attic, but this time felt different.

He felt like he was drawn to something, and it was the attic that drew Jean-Pierre's thoughts like a moth to a flame. Guarded by a heavy wooden door that groaned in protest as his father opened it, the attic was a vast space that held the traces of time in its embrace. Sunlight filtered through a circular window, casting a dim, ethereal glow upon the scattered remnants of the past—a faded tapestry hung askew, dusty suitcases stacked haphazardly, and the remnants of children's toys long abandoned. Cobwebs draped over a stack of boxes, and an old rocking horse, once played on by Jean-Pierre and Chantelle and Marcel and who knows how many others, stood in a corner.

"Ah," Marcel said with a nostalgic chuckle as he saw the rocking horse. "Perhaps the children would enjoy this."

Jean-Pierre smiled. "Even that has a story to tell," he said, running his hand over the worn wooden seat, remembering his childhood and how he would rock it so hard.

The attic was a relic of the past, a space forgotten by time, and Jean-Pierre stood for a moment, taking it all in. He saw the dust hang in the air as it was illuminated by beams of sunlight streaming through the small, grime-covered window. His anticipation up to this point was mingled with trepidation. The attic was a shrine to forgotten stories, echoing the struggles of those who had come before him. Here, beneath the eaves, he could almost feel the presence of a Dupont and the other Resistance fighters who had traversed the dangerous roads of wartime France. Was the Dupont mentioned a Resistance fighter? he thought to himself. He looked at the area and thought this could have been a space where plans had been laid, lives had been risked, and hope had flickered defiantly against the backdrop of despair.

Jean-Pierre seemed to be in a trance and slowly moved deeper into the attic, navigating the jumble of objects that had been left to gather dust. His fingers brushed against a weathered trunk, its leather cracked and worn. Inside, there might be remnants of letters and photographs that hinted at lives intertwined with the Resistance. Each document felt like a lost thread in the tapestry of history, waiting for him to pull and unravel the stories contained within.

Though enticing, this space was tinged with a heavy weight. It was more than just an attic full of memories; it was a symbol of his family's legacy and the burdens that came with diving into their past.

What if I disturb something better left alone?

Those nagging thoughts crept back into his mind, threading through his excitement. The attic stood not only as a repository of memories but as a reminder of the risks inherent in seeking the truth. He remembered Chantelle's words *Be careful what you look for!*

Bookshelves lined one wall, collapsing under the weight of dusty volumes recounting battles waged, sacrifices made, and heroes lost. Jean-Pierre realised that a specific Dupont had once roamed these very floors, drafting letters, organising operations, and forging bonds of loyalty amidst the uncertainty of war. Each text was a testament to courage, but also to the cost of that courage—a price he now felt drawn to unravel.

As he lingered among the relics, Jean-Pierre experienced an overwhelming sense of responsibility settle upon his shoulders. Uncovering this story would require more than mere curiosity; it demanded respect and courage to face whatever truths lay hidden within these walls. The attic, once a mere storage space, transformed into a sanctuary of heritage—a reminder that the past echoes into the present, shaping who he was and who he might become.

With renewed urgency, he began to sift through the remnants more carefully, feeling as though he was partaking in a dialogue with those who had come before him. Here, amid the dust and shadows, Jean-Pierre understood that he wasn't merely chasing a legacy; he was being called to honour it, to breathe life into the stories abandoned in the quiet corners of the château, and to confront the burdens that history had left him.

"Come on Jean-Pierre!" remarked Marcel, "let's start with those boxes," he said pointing to the cobweb-covered stack.

The two rummaged through the boxes, one by one, carefully uncovering forgotten items—children's toys, faded photographs, and old clothing. Marcel held up a pair of baby shoes, his expression softening with memory.

"*Papa*," Jean-Pierre reminded gently, "we're here for the letters."

"Of course," Marcel said, snapping back to the task at hand.

At the far corner of the attic, a wooden chest caught Marcel's eye. It was hidden beneath a stack of chairs and a pile of old blankets. Marcel worked to clear the area, and with Jean-Pierre's help, he dragged the chest into the centre of the room.

The chest creaked as Marcel lifted the lid, revealing a jumble of blankets and linens. He carefully moved them aside, and beneath the fabric was a small shoebox tied with twine. Marcel lifted it reverently and placed it on the floor between them.

Inside were dozens of letters, their edges yellowed with age. Marcel picked one up, scanning its delicate handwriting. Jean-Pierre leaned closer, his heart pounding.

"Look at this," he said, holding up a letter with strange markings. "What language is that, *Papa*?"

Marcel studied the page, his eyes narrowed in concentration. "It's not a language—it's a code," he murmured, his mind racing. "A secret code."

Jean-Pierre's eyes lit up. "We may be onto something here, *Papa*. Do you think it may be French Resistance?"

***

Back in the kitchen, Marcel and Jean-Pierre placed the shoebox on the table. Genevieve, seeing their dishevelled appearance, laughed.

"Well, it looks like you two have been in the dungeons," she teased.

"*Maman*, we found something incredible," Jean-Pierre said. "Letters—cryptic ones. We're going to work through them now."

Genevieve's curiosity was piqued. "Ooh, that sounds like fun. Can I join in?"

The three of them cleared the table, setting aside the morning's breakfast dishes to make room for their investigation. Marcel brewed another pot of coffee, and they began spreading the letters out across the table.

The letters were fragile, written in neat but cryptic handwriting. Marcel, ever methodical, suggested they sort them by date and appearance, looking for patterns. Genevieve joined in, her keen eye spotting recurring symbols.

"Look at us," Marcel said with a smile, glancing at his wife. "Here we go again, researching and deciphering, just like old times." Genevieve smiled back warmly, the memory of their university days flashing in her mind. "We do make a good team," she said.

Jean-Pierre watched his parents work together; their bond evident in the way they moved in harmony. It was a moment he cherished, a glimpse of the partnership that had built not only their family but their legacy.

***

As the morning turned to afternoon, they began to see faint patterns in the code—repeated symbols and numbers that suggested some kind of key. Marcel speculated that the letters might contain instructions or messages from the Resistance.

"Whoever wrote these," Marcel said, "was taking great care to keep their secrets safe. If these are Resistance documents, they could be incredibly significant."

Genevieve nodded, her finger tracing a series of numbers on one of the pages. "Do you think your parents knew about these?"

Marcel shrugged. "I'm not sure. But I think this is just the beginning."

As they continued to work, the room filled with a sense of purpose. The letters, once a mystery, began to feel like a bridge to the past—a connection to the courage and perseverance of those who had come before them.

And though the code remained unsolved for now, one thing was clear: the Dupont family had a story to tell, and Jean-Pierre was determined to uncover it.

* * *

Jean-Pierre arrived home to the usual chorus of joyful shouts. *"Papa!"* Giselle and Pascal rushed to him; their small arms outstretched. With a child swooped up in each arm, Jean-Pierre kissed Ana, who stood in the doorway with a radiant smile. The four of them shared a warm group hug, a perfect moment of family unity.

Ana's laughter rang out, her joy infectious as she watched her husband and children. "Come on, everyone," she said, leading them inside. "Let's get dinner started."

Jean-Pierre followed her into the kitchen, setting the kids down at the table where they each received a glass of freshly poured grape juice. Ana began chopping vegetables while Jean-Pierre joined her, picking up a knife to help.

As they worked together, Jean-Pierre recounted his day. "You should have seen the attic," he began, his voice tinged with both amusement and nostalgia. "It's been untouched for years—dust, cobwebs, and old treasures everywhere."

"Was it scary, *Papa*?" Giselle asked, her big eyes wide with wonder.

Jean-Pierre chuckled. "Only if you're afraid of spiders," he teased, making Pascal squirm and giggle.

"What were you doing up there?" Ana asked, curious.

Jean-Pierre explained about the cryptic letters and how he, Marcel, and Genevieve had worked together to decipher them. "They seem to be linked to the French Resistance," he said, his excitement detectable.

"That sounds difficult," Ana said, her knife pausing mid-chop. "Where do you even start?"

Jean-Pierre grinned. "It is challenging. But my parents are brilliant. They taught me how to look for patterns, repetitions, and organise everything into a system. Once you start cracking parts of the code, the message begins to reveal itself."

"What did the letters say, *Papa*?" Giselle asked, her curiosity unbridled.

"We don't know yet," Jean-Pierre admitted. "But I uncovered Louis Dupont's name and I'm not too sure if it's grandad or possibly another family member. He may be a brother or relative. I'll need to dig deeper to find out more."

Ana's hands stilled, her expression turning serious. "Jean-Pierre," she said softly, "are you sure you want to dig so much?"

Jean-Pierre looked at her, startled. "What do you mean?"

Ana set down her knife and turned to face him, her voice measured. "I love how passionate you are about your family's history. I think it's wonderful that you want to honour your heritage. But... what if you uncover something unsettling? Something you'd rather not know?"

Jean-Pierre frowned, trying to understand her concern. "Ana, learning about our past inspires me. It makes me want to achieve more and carry on the family's legacy."

Ana's eyes glistened with unshed tears. "I know, my love. But I just want peace and harmony in this house. I'm afraid of anything that might disrupt that."

Jean-Pierre's heart sank. They had never argued before, and the tension between them now felt unfamiliar and unsettling. He reached for her hand, squeezing it gently.

"I promise you," he said, his voice steady, "our home will always be a place of love and tranquillity. I'll be careful with what I uncover and share. Our family comes first."

Ana nodded, a small smile returning to her lips. She kissed his cheek before turning back to the stove.

***

After dinner, Ana tucked Giselle and Pascal into bed. They kissed Jean-Pierre goodnight, their sleepy voices murmuring, *"Bonne nuit, Papa."*

Jean-Pierre poured himself a glass of Cabernet Franc and settled into an armchair by the fire. The flickering flames cast dancing shadows on the walls as he sipped the wine and reflected on Ana's words. Her concerns weighed heavily on him. Was he being selfish? He thought of Chantelle's warning: *"Be careful, big brother. You may not like what you find."*

What if his pursuit of the past brought unintended consequences? What if it caused pain or disrupted the harmony of their family? Jean-Pierre resolved to tread carefully. He would pursue the truth but with discretion, sharing only what would bring pride and understanding. For now, he needed to reassure Ana of his commitment to their family's happiness.

He set down his glass and went to find her. She was in their bedroom, getting ready for bed. Without a word, Jean-Pierre wrapped his arms around her from behind, resting his chin on her shoulder.

"I'm sorry," he murmured.

Ana turned to face him, her expression soft. "There's nothing to apologise for," she said.

"There is," Jean-Pierre insisted. "I don't want to hurt anyone, least of all you. I'll be careful, I promise."

Ana smiled and placed a hand on his cheek. "I trust you, Jean-Pierre. Just remember, our family is what matters most."

Jean-Pierre nodded, kissing her forehead. "Always."

***

As Jean-Pierre lay in bed that night, his mind returned to the name Louis Dupont. Who was he? Was it Marcel's father, his granddad and what role had he played in the French Resistance?

Tomorrow, he would go back to the library and search for answers. But tonight, he was content to hold Ana close, her steady breaths a reminder of what was truly important.

The past could wait until morning.

Chapter 10

Jean-Pierre wasted no time diving into his research the next morning. He headed straight to the library, armed with determination and a notebook. His focus was to uncover everything he could about Louis Dupont and his role in the French Resistance during World War II.

The archives were a maze of aged documents and brittle pages, but Jean-Pierre navigated them with precision. He began by searching through local records and historical accounts of the Resistance in the region. After hours of combing through material, he found his first breakthrough: a brief mention of a *Louis Dupont*, listed as a known member of a Resistance cell operating near Lyon.

Excited, Jean-Pierre remembered his father's stories about the bravery of the Resistance fighters, risking their lives to undermine the German occupation. Marcel had always spoken of them with reverence, and Jean-Pierre now felt a renewed urgency to uncover Louis's contributions.

Further research revealed that Louis had been involved in the distribution of secret letters—messages that were critical to coordinating Resistance efforts. Some of these letters were rumoured to have been hidden in safe houses, their locations lost over time.

Jean-Pierre's heart raced. Could the letters in the château's attic be among those?

References to nearby villages and a small town kept recurring in his search. These places seemed to be key to Louis's activities. Jean-Pierre jotted down the names, feeling both a sense of accomplishment and an overwhelming flood of information. Saturated and mentally drained, he decided to leave the library and visit one of the villages mentioned in the documents.

***

The drive to the village was peaceful at first, the winding country roads lined with trees glowing golden in the late afternoon sun. But soon, Jean-Pierre noticed a black car in his rearview mirror. It had been behind him for several kilometres, keeping a steady distance.

At first, he dismissed the idea that he was being followed. But as the kilometres stretched on, his unease grew. The car's persistence felt deliberate.

Spotting a service station up ahead, Jean-Pierre decided to stop and test his suspicion. Pulling into the parking lot, he noticed the black car slow down and pull in behind him, parking a few spaces away.

Jean-Pierre's heart pounded. He walked into the café attached to the station, ordered a coffee, and stood at a small table near the window, pretending to be absorbed in his drink. His eyes, however, stayed fixed on the black car.

The vehicle's occupants didn't emerge, their silhouettes barely visible through the tinted windows. Jean-Pierre's mind raced. Who were they? Why were they following him? He had no answers, only a growing sense of dread.

Finishing his coffee, he had no choice but to return to his car. Steeling himself, he walked out and climbed into the driver's seat, starting the engine. He decided to take an indirect route back to the main road, turning into the side streets of the small town.

His instincts were right—the black car followed. Turning left, then right, and then right again, he tried to lose them. But as he accelerated back onto the main road, the car reappeared in his rearview mirror.

Jean-Pierre's chest tightened with fear, his thoughts a blur. He couldn't risk leading them back to the château and his family. As the road curved, he pushed his car faster, overtaking a slower vehicle. A horn blared as an oncoming car swerved to avoid him.

As Jean-Pierre's heart raced with the roar of his engine, his mind spiralled through a cacophony of thoughts. Each tight turn he made sent adrenaline flooding his veins, sharpening his senses.

Why are they following me? What do they know? The questions clawed at him as he focused on the road ahead. The black car loomed in his rearview mirror, a dark shadow that seemed to mock his every attempt to escape. He could almost feel their eyes scrutinising him, waiting for him to make a mistake.

He turned right, then left, praying his instincts would be enough to outsmart whoever was behind him. *Think, Jean-Pierre, think!* He recalled the dusty paths off the main road he'd explored as a child, weaving between the trees. The countryside was his playground— yet now it felt like a maze he had to get to and navigate while an unseen predator stalked him.

Focus on the bends, he reminded himself as he tightened his grip on the steering wheel, feeling the familiar nudge of fatigue battling against his determination. The previous car that swerved on the bend and barely missed him, was maybe too close for comfort. He knew that in this moment, panic could betray him. Every decision counted. The farmhouse gate flashed in his mind—a quick route away from his pursuers. *It's now or never.*

He saw it, and as he veered onto the gravel driveway, the world outside blurred. His breath came in shallow gasps, each one reminding him of the children waiting at home, the weight of his family's safety pressing heavily on his chest. *What would Ana think? What would she say if something happened to me?* The thought sent a jolt through him, urging him to push harder and drive faster. He couldn't allow fear to dictate his actions. He found a shed and tucked in behind it, his heart pounding as he looked through the trees lining the property and watched the road.

When the black car shot past, a rush of relief flooded him, but it was immediately tempered by the gnawing uncertainty of their intentions. *What if they turn around? What if they're laying in wait?* His instincts urged him to remain cautious. He waited, counting heartbeats, praying that the dust settling around him would be the curtain that kept his family from danger.

A surge of clarity pierced through the chaos: he couldn't let this investigation put them at risk. The chase wasn't just about him anymore; it was about protecting his family and honouring the legacy he was trying to uncover. *Find the truth, but be smart about it,* he silently vowed.

When he finally backtracked to the town, taking extra care to note every turn and landmark, his thoughts danced dangerously close to despair. He felt the weight of every secret uncovered, every piece of history threatening to unravel the life he had built with Ana and the children.

Conscious of time slipping away, he accelerated into the distance, each passing moment solidifying his resolve. The pursuit had ignited a flame within him—one that was both terrifying and exhilarating.

In the midst of every inch of fear he clung to, a new determination emerged. Pushing aside his anxious thoughts, he whispered to himself, *For them, I will find the truth.* The shadows of the past might threaten, but he refused to back down.

***

As Jean-Pierre parked his car outside the cottage adjacent to the château, he sat for a moment, his thoughts racing. Perhaps Ana was right. Perhaps he was delving too deep into something better left alone. But a part of him rebelled against the idea. He wanted to know more—to honour the legacy of the château and the efforts of his forefathers.

His musings were interrupted by the sound of small feet running towards the car. Giselle and Pascal, having heard him arrive, came rushing out with squeals of delight. Jean-Pierre stepped out, scooped them up, and carried them into the house.

Ana greeted him with a warm smile and a kiss. "How was your day, *mon cher*?" she asked, her tone light.

Jean-Pierre hesitated. "Fine," he said, forcing a smile. "I found a few more documents."

Unease tugged at him. He hated being dishonest with Ana but didn't want to burden her with what had happened. He set the children down in the kitchen and poured himself a glass of homemade lemon juice, his mind still racing.

Later, at the dinner table, Ana gave him a concerned look. "Are you alright, *mon cher*? You seem a bit off."

Jean-Pierre forced a laugh. "Just tired," he said. "I think all this research is exhausting me."

Ana placed her hand on his. "Why don't we take a break tomorrow? Let's visit the village as a family."

Giselle's eyes lit up. "Please, *Papa*! Let's go to the village!" she begged, bouncing in her seat.

Pascal joined in, giggling and clapping his hands. "Please, *Papa*! Please!"

Jean-Pierre smiled at their enthusiasm, his heart softening. "Alright," he said. "We'll go to the village."

But deep down, he couldn't shake the events of the day. The shadow of the black car lingered in his mind, a silent warning that his search for the truth might come at a cost.

Mario Zatta

Chapter 11

The morning at the cottage was alive with energy. Giselle and Pascal were bursting with excitement, darting back and forth from the breakfast table to their rooms to grab jackets, gloves, and scarves.

"Let's go! Let's go!" they shouted in unison, their voices echoing through the house.

"Finish your breakfast, or we're not going anywhere!" Jean-Pierre called after them, his voice carrying a blend of authority and amusement.

At last, the children hurried back, shovelling the rest of their breakfast while Ana made sure everyone was bundled up against the winter chill. Jackets were zipped, boots laced, and scarves snugly wrapped. Finally, the family piled into the car and set off for the village.

***

The local village was bustling with activity. The winter market had drawn residents and visitors alike, and the air was filled with the mingling scents of fresh pastries, mulled wine, and roasted chestnuts. Vendors lined the cobblestone streets, their stalls decorated with pine boughs, red ribbons, and glowing lanterns. Snow dusted the rooftops and crunched underfoot, adding to the festive atmosphere.

Giselle and Pascal darted between stalls, their eyes wide with wonder. Jean-Pierre and Ana strolled behind them, pointing out the various offerings.

"Look at these," Jean-Pierre said, crouching to show Giselle a display of handcrafted wooden toys. "These are made from local chestnut trees. Did you know your grandfather used to make things like this when he was young?"

Giselle beamed, running her fingers over a finely carved horse. "Can we get one, *Papa*?"

"We'll see," Jean-Pierre said with a smile.

At another stall, Ana showed Pascal jars of golden honey. "This comes from the bees in the valley," she explained. "When I was a little girl, my mother would buy a jar, and we'd spread it on warm bread after school."

Pascal's eyes lit up. "Can we do that too, *Maman*?"

"Of course," Ana said, ruffling his hair.

The family wandered through stalls selling colourful woollen scarves, intricate lacework, and fragrant candles. They sampled *vin chaud* (mulled wine for the adults) and *chocolat chaud* (hot chocolate) for the children. Nearby, a vendor offered freshly baked *kouglof*, a traditional Alsatian brioche studded with dried fruits and dusted with powdered sugar.

"This is a winter specialty," Jean-Pierre explained, breaking off a piece for Giselle to try. "It's been made in this region for hundreds of years."

"It's delicious!" Giselle exclaimed, licking the sugar from her fingers.

Halfway through their visit, Ana's eyes lit up as she spotted a cooking demonstration in the square. A chef, dressed in a crisp white coat, was teaching villagers how to prepare traditional winter dishes. Children gathered around tables piled with dough, bowls of filling, and cookie cutters shaped like stars and bells.

"Let's join!" Ana said, tugging on Jean-Pierre's arm.

Giselle and Pascal eagerly followed, and soon the family was elbow-deep in flour and butter. Under the chef's guidance, they rolled out dough, shaped cookies, and filled tarts with spiced apples. Ana worked with a gleam of joy in her eyes, guiding the children with patient hands.

Jean-Pierre stood to the side, smiling as he watched.

"That looks perfect, Giselle!" he called out. "Good job, Pascal!"

As they worked, Jean-Pierre's attention drifted to the neighbouring stall. An old man sat there, bundled in a thick coat and cap, selling jars of preserves and winter vegetables. His face was weathered, with deep lines etched by time, and his eyes held a quiet wisdom.

Curious, Jean-Pierre approached the man. *"Bonjour, monsieur,"* he said. "Beautiful market today, isn't it?"

The old man looked up and smiled. "Indeed, young man. It's good to see the village alive like this."

Jean-Pierre leaned on the edge of the stall. "You've lived here long?"

"All my life," the man said. "This village is my home. I've seen it change over the years—through the war, the rebuilding, and now."

Jean-Pierre's pulse quickened. "The war... Did you live here during that time?"

The man nodded, his weathered face clouding with memories, his voice lowering as if sharing a sacred tale. "I was just a boy when the Germans came," he began, his words heavy with emotion. "We had no choice but to grow up fast back then. Childhood was a luxury we couldn't afford, not when every day brought new dangers. The village became a different place overnight—quiet, watchful, like a forest holding its breath. Fear was everywhere, but so was resolve."

He paused, his gaze drifting to the horizon as if he could still see the shadows of that time. "Everyone had a role to play, no matter their age. Some hid our neighbours—people who would have vanished if the Germans found them. Others risked their lives carrying messages, knowing one mistake could mean death for them and their families. Even keeping the farms running was an act of defiance. The food we grew didn't just feed us; it kept the resistance alive. Every loaf of bread, every basket of potatoes, was a lifeline smuggled into the hills where they hid."

His voice faltered, and he swallowed hard, his hands trembling slightly as they rested on the table. "It wasn't easy," he continued, his eyes locking with Jean-Pierre's. "We faced betrayal, hunger, and the constant threat of discovery. But through it all, we stood together. The bonds we formed in those dark days—they were unbreakable. We didn't just survive; we endured, for each other and for the hope that one day the world would be different."

The man sighed deeply, his voice softening. "That hope is what kept us going. And sometimes, when I see the young ones laughing and playing in the market, I think—yes, it was worth it. Everything we did, every risk we took, was for them." He looked at Jean-Pierre with a penetrating gaze. "But it came at a cost, and not all stories are meant to be uncovered, lad. Some truths are heavier than they seem." Jean-Pierre hesitated, then asked, "Did you know a man named Louis Dupont?"

The old man's eyes narrowed as he studied Jean-Pierre carefully. "Why do you ask?"

"He was my ancestor," Jean-Pierre admitted. "I've been researching my family's history, and his name keeps coming up."

The man's gaze softened. "Ah, Louis... Yes, I knew him. He was one of the brave ones. He did things most of us wouldn't dare to. The good he did for this village... It's hard to put into words."

"What kind of things?" Jean-Pierre pressed.

The man hesitated, glancing around as if ensuring no one was listening. "He was part of the Resistance. He helped save lives, smuggled people out, and disrupted the enemy's plans. But those were dangerous times. Many secrets were kept, even from friends. Be careful, young man. Sometimes digging too deep can stir up things best left buried."

Before Jean-Pierre could ask more, Ana's voice rang out. "Jean-Pierre! Come here!"

Giselle ran up to him, holding a beautifully decorated cookie. "I made this for you, *Papa*!" she said proudly.

Jean-Pierre knelt and took the treat, pulling her into a hug. "Thank you, my sweet girl. It's perfect."

As Ana and Pascal joined them, Jean-Pierre looked back at the old man, who gave him a knowing nod.
"Enjoy the market," the man said quietly. "And take care."

Jean-Pierre walked back to his family, the taste of the cookie mingling with the weight of the old man's words.

Mario Zatta

Chapter 12

The soft glow of the afternoon sun filtered through the vineyard's bare winter vines as Jean-Pierre sat in the château's study. Surrounding him were stacks of old documents, books, and photographs, each one a fragment of his family's history. His eyes were drawn to an envelope marked with faded ink, its edges worn and delicate from time.

Inside, he found a letter written in French, its neat handwriting betraying a sense of urgency. The contents seemed ordinary at first glance, detailing shipments of wine and mundane updates from a time long past. But something caught Jean-Pierre's eye—a series of seemingly random letters and numbers scattered throughout the text. He grabbed a notebook and began jotting them down, arranging and rearranging the characters in search of a pattern. Hours passed, and the room grew colder, but Jean-Pierre didn't notice. His focus sharpened as the scattered symbols aligned to form a phrase:

"For Jacques Lambert. Trust only the stars."

The name stirred a vague memory from his research earlier in the week. Jacques Lambert was mentioned briefly in war-era records as an enigmatic figure associated with the French Resistance. The connection to Louis Dupont, however, was unexpected. Why would Louis, his great-grandfather, address this cryptic message to a man seemingly outside the family?

Jean-Pierre felt a rush of excitement mixed with unease. The coded message hinted at a clandestine relationship between Louis Dupont and Jacques Lambert, one that may hold answers to questions he didn't yet know to ask.

Seeking insight, Jean-Pierre called Marcel into the study. His father appeared moments later, holding a steaming mug of coffee.
"What's this about, Jean?" Marcel asked, setting the mug down.

Jean-Pierre explained the discovery, his words tumbling over one another as he described the coded letter and its implications. Marcel listened intently, his sharp mind already drawing connections.

"This phrase—'trust only the stars'—is intriguing," Marcel mused, leaning over the desk. "It could refer to navigation, perhaps astronomical symbols used by the Resistance to communicate in secret. Or, it could be something metaphorical—trusting one's instincts or a trusted guide."

Jean-Pierre nodded, inspired by his father's interpretation. The conversation deepened, weaving through history, astronomy, and family. Marcel mentioned that Louis Dupont's involvement in the Resistance was always shrouded in secrecy, even within the family. Jean-Pierre nodded as Marcel leaned back in his chair, his gaze fixed on the crackling fire in the study's hearth. The flickering flames seemed to draw out memories as he began to speak, his voice tinged with both reverence and solemnity.

"My father Louis Dupont was always a figure of mystery," Marcel began, folding his hands thoughtfully. "Even my grandfather, Charles, spoke of him rarely and with great caution. Also as a child, I could sense that there was something unspoken, a history too dangerous or painful to share freely. The Resistance—" Marcel paused, his voice lowering slightly, "it wasn't just about fighting the enemy. It was about navigating a world where trust was a precious, fleeting thing. Secrets weren't just a habit; they were a necessity. Even within the family."

He shifted his gaze to Jean-Pierre, his hazel eyes intense. "My grandfather, Charles, was a man of reason, much like you. But when it came to Louis, he carried a burden of unanswered questions. Louis kept so much of his involvement hidden. Charles once told me that Louis would leave the house at odd hours without explanation. He'd return days later, battered and weary, but when questioned, he'd deflect—always with the same reply: *'It's better that you don't know.'*"

Jean-Pierre listened intently, the gravity of his father's words sinking in. "Why do you think he was so determined to keep everyone in the dark?"

Marcel sighed, his expression grave. "To protect us. The Resistance was a deadly game, Jean-Pierre. Information was currency and knowing too much could make you a target—not just for the enemy, but for collaborators and traitors. Even after the war, those habits of secrecy lingered. My grandfather respected that, but it also frustrated him deeply. He wanted to understand, to connect with Louis on a deeper level, but the wall of silence was impenetrable."

His voice softened as he continued. "And yet, there was pride—an immense pride. My grandfather would sometimes speak of Louis's courage, though never in detail. He'd say things like, *'Your father did what was needed to be done, no matter the cost.'* That's the legacy Louis left behind: a legacy of sacrifice, resilience, and love for his family, even if it came at the cost of openness."

Marcel leaned forward, his tone growing more reflective. "But secrecy takes its toll. My grandfather always carried a sense of distance from Louis, a gap he could never quite bridge. I think he resented it at times, even as he understood it. It created a strange duality—pride in Louis's heroism, but frustration with the shadow it cast over our family's understanding of who he truly was."

Jean-Pierre absorbed his father's words, a profound respect settling over him. "Do you think Louis ever regretted keeping those secrets? That he wished he could share more?"

Marcel smiled faintly, a glimmer of warmth breaking through the weight of the conversation. "I'd like to think so. Secrets protect, but they also isolate. Perhaps, in his own way, Louis hoped someone like you would come along—someone with the patience to piece together the fragments and the courage to uncover the truth."

The room fell into a contemplative silence, the fire's soft crackle filling the space. Jean-Pierre felt a renewed sense of purpose, not just for himself but for the generations that had come before. He realised that uncovering the truth about Louis Dupont wasn't just an investigation—it was a chance to bridge the gaps left by secrecy and honour the resilience that carried his family through history.

***

Later that evening, the family gathered around the dining table in the warm glow of the chandelier, the scent of roasted lamb and fresh bread filling the room. As they passed the plates around, Jean-Pierre could feel the weight of his discovery pressing on him. He was eager to share what he had uncovered, but he knew the conversation wouldn't be easy. His sister Chantelle, ever the voice of reason, noticed the intensity in his eyes before he spoke.

"I found something today," Jean-Pierre began, setting down his glass of wine. His fingers twitched slightly as he pulled the folded letter from his pocket, the cryptic message inside still fresh in his mind. He looked at both Chantelle and Adrien. "It ties Louis Dupont to Jacques Lambert—and potentially to the French Resistance. There's a code in the letter. I think we've stumbled onto something much bigger than we anticipated."

Chantelle raised an eyebrow, her green eyes flickering with concern. She leaned back in her chair, her tone measured but firm. "Jean-Pierre, I understand your curiosity. You've always been driven to uncover the truth. But I worry…" She paused, carefully choosing her words. "You're treading on dangerous ground. The past has a way of consuming people, and I don't want to see you lose sight of what's important in the present. What we discover about Louis or the Resistance won't change the here and now."

Her words lingered in the air, a quiet warning that cut through Jean-Pierre's excitement. She continued, her voice soft but insistent. "Our family's lived with those secrets for generations. There's a reason why your grandfather kept them hidden. Maybe some truths are better left in the past. I don't want to see you become obsessed with it all—not at the cost of your own peace of mind, or the family."

Jean-Pierre met her gaze, the weight of her concern sinking in. He knew she was right—Chantelle's voice had always been grounded in practicality, and she had seen the toll that obsession with the past could take. Still, his sense of duty to uncover the truth pushed him forward. He opened his mouth to respond, but Adrien cut in before he could speak.

Adrien, ever the pragmatist, looked at Jean-Pierre with a steady gaze, his voice calm but filled with conviction. "Chantelle has a point, Jean-Pierre. You're uncovering something incredible, yes, but remember what you're dealing with. History is a double-edged sword—it can illuminate, but it can also cast shadows."

He leaned forward, resting his elbows on the table, his hands clasped together. "What you're discovering—your grandfather's connections, the role he played—it's important, but it has consequences. The past doesn't just live in textbooks. It shapes the present in ways we can't always predict. What if there are people still out there who don't want this story to come to light? What if this investigation puts our family in danger?"

Adrien's words hit harder than Jean-Pierre expected. He'd been so focused on the pieces of the puzzle he'd uncovered that he hadn't fully considered the risks. Adrien's pragmatism always had a way of cutting through the excitement and reminding Jean-Pierre of the larger picture.

"I'm not saying you shouldn't pursue this," Adrien continued, his voice softening. "But you need to think about how far you're willing to go. There are things about your family's past—things about your family's legacy—that may have been buried for a reason. Sometimes, uncovering the truth is worth the risk. But you should be prepared for what might come with it."

Jean-Pierre looked at both of them—his sister's caution and Adrien's calculated perspective. He knew they were both right. He felt the weight of their words settle into him, and for the first time, a flicker of doubt crossed his mind. What if the truth he's chasing comes at too high a cost? What if he's already gone too far to turn back?

The conversation lingered, the room quiet except for the crackling of the fire in the hearth. Jean-Pierre sat back in his chair, taking a long breath, the path ahead now seemed less clear than before. His search for answers had become more than just a quest for knowledge—it was a journey fraught with uncertainty, and the stakes were higher than he ever imagined.

Jean-Pierre felt the weight of their words but remained resolute. The coded letter had reignited his determination to piece together the puzzle of his family's past. He knew the road ahead would be fraught with challenges, but the promise of understanding the connection between Louis Dupont and Jacques Lambert was a mystery too compelling to ignore.

As the night fell over the château, Jean-Pierre sat alone in his study, the letter in one hand and a glass of wine in the other. Just like his father, he glanced out the window at the stars, their faint light a reminder of the phrase in the letter. For the first time in weeks, he felt a sense of clarity—both the stars above and the ancestors below seemed to guide him towards the truth.

Mario Zatta

Chapter 13

The morning light filtered through the château's dining room as the family gathered for breakfast. The aroma of freshly brewed coffee mingled with the scent of warm croissants and fruit preserves. Jean-Pierre had barely touched his plate, his mind preoccupied with the coded letter and its implications.

After several minutes of silence, he cleared his throat. "I thought all night about what you said. However, I found something else—something important."

Chantelle set her cup down, her green eyes narrowing in curiosity. "What is it?"

Jean-Pierre reached into his pocket and retrieved the same letter, carefully unfolding it. The room fell silent as he placed it on the table. Chantelle leaned in, her brow lined as she studied the faded text and the decoded message. Adrien, sitting beside her, glanced between them with interest.

"This phrase," Jean-Pierre began, pointing to the decoded portion, "'For Jacques Lambert. Trust only the stars.' It not only connects

Louis Dupont to the French Resistance but it's coded *Don't trust anyone*. And Jacques Lambert—his name wasn't in anything else I've found so far. He's an unknown."

Chantelle's fingers hovered over the paper, again wary of what she didn't understand. "Jean, this is fascinating, but again, it's cryptic. You don't know where it leads or what kind of consequences it could have."

Adrien nodded thoughtfully. "She's right. You're digging into a past that might not want to be uncovered. What if this Lambert was involved in something dangerous? What if uncovering this connection puts us—your family—in harm's way?"

Jean-Pierre's jaw tightened, his voice carrying the weight of his conviction. "I can't ignore this. If Louis was part of something bigger, if our family played a role in history, I need to know. We need to know. This is about understanding who we are and where we come from."

Chantelle exhaled slowly, her expression softening. "I understand why this is important to you, and I don't want to repeat myself, but you need to think about your family now—your children, and Ana.

You're not just uncovering stories; you're potentially stirring up conflicts. People don't leave cryptic codes for no reason."

Adrien placed a reassuring hand on Jean-Pierre's shoulder. "Your sister's right, but so are you. There's value in knowing our past, but you can't let it consume you. Balance is key. Keep digging, but don't let it come at the cost of your present."

Jean-Pierre's gaze shifted to the window, where his children were playing outside, their laughter ringing through the crisp winter air. His expression softened, and a hint of doubt crept into his voice. "I know I need to be careful, but this feels… important. Like it's something I'm meant to do."

Chantelle stood and walked over to him. "Then promise us this: don't take unnecessary risks. If you find yourself in dangerous territory, step back. Your family needs you."

Adrien added, "And don't be afraid to ask for help. You're not in this alone, Jean. We'll support you, but we'll also remind you when it's time to step back."

Jean-Pierre nodded, gratitude flickering in his hazel eyes. "Thank you. Both of you. I'll tread carefully, but I won't stop until I find the truth."

The conversation shifted to lighter topics as the family finished breakfast, but Jean-Pierre's mind remained on the letter and the questions it raised. As the day unfolded, he felt the weight of responsibility to balance his investigation with the life he had built— a delicate act of honouring the past while protecting the future.

* * *

That afternoon, Jean-Pierre stepped into the vineyard with his children, Giselle and Pascal. The winter sun filtered through the lattice of leafless vines, casting a soft warm light over the rows. The air was crisp, the ground beneath his boots firm from the lingering frost. Giselle darted between the dormant vines, her laughter echoing like bells, while Pascal scrambled after her, determined to keep up with his sister.

"*Papa*, watch me!" Giselle called, her voice full of energy. She balanced precariously on a low post, arms stretched wide like a tightrope walker. Jean-Pierre smiled faintly, clapping his hands in encouragement. Pascal, giggling uncontrollably, attempted to imitate her but slipped into the grass, laughing even harder.

Ana stood near the edge of the vineyard, watching the scene with quiet contentment. Seeing Jean-Pierre out here with the children brought her joy. It felt like a rare, precious moment when the weight on his shoulders seemed to lift, even if only slightly.

Jean-Pierre continued to watch his children play, his gaze softening. They reminded him of himself and Chantelle as children, running through these same rows, playing hide-and-seek amidst the vines. He could almost hear the echoes of their childhood laughter blending with Giselle's and Pascal's, a bittersweet harmony that tugged at his heart.

Yet, even in this moment, part of him felt distant. Though he stood in the vineyard he cherished, surrounded by the family he loves, they all seemed shrouded in a fog. His mind drifted to the letter, the cryptic words, and the puzzle they had left him to solve. He looked out over the rows of vines stretching into the horizon and then turned his gaze towards the château.

The stone façade rose majestically, a testament to the Dupont legacy. The towering structure stood firm against the backdrop of the Alps, their snow-capped peaks glinting in the sunlight. The château had stood for generations, its walls keeping the stories of those who came before him.

"I'll find out," he whispered to himself, his voice low but resolute. "I want to know everything about you."

A sharp, joyful cry broke his reverie. "*Papa*! *Papa*!" Giselle's voice pulled him back, and he turned just in time to see her sprinting towards him, her cheeks flushed from the cold. Pascal was right behind her, scrambling and giggling as he tried to catch up.

Jean-Pierre knelt, opening his arms as Giselle crashed into him, wrapping her tiny arms around his neck. Pascal tumbled in next, clinging to his father's leg, still laughing. Jean-Pierre hugged them both tightly, feeling their warmth seep into him.

Ana approached; her smile radiant. "They've been waiting all morning for you to join them," she said softly, her hand resting on his shoulder.

Jean-Pierre glanced up at her and nodded, the fog momentarily lifting. For now, he is here, with them, holding on to the moment before the questions of the past pull him away again.

Chapter 14

Jean-Pierre sat in his study, surrounded by stacks of papers, historical texts, and an array of handwritten notes. The coded message lay on the desk before him, its cryptic letters daring him to unlock their secret. The room was bathed in the soft glow of a desk lamp, the only light illuminating the late evening. Outside, the winds whispered through the vineyard, a faint echo of the past seeming to murmur in his ears.

The message had haunted him since he first laid eyes on it. Written in Louis Dupont's unmistakable script, the letter bore a cypher that Jean-Pierre had struggled to crack for days. Each attempt seemed to lead to another dead end, another piece of history left tantalisingly out of reach. But tonight felt different. Tonight, he was determined to break through.

He stared at the coded text, his mind tracing over its repetitive patterns. The letters appeared random at first glance, but Jean-Pierre knew better. Louis had been a man of precision, his actions deliberate. There was a method to this madness—he just needed to find it.

Jean-Pierre's thoughts drifted to his father's words from the previous evening, a reminder of the secrecy surrounding Louis's life. "Secrecy was his shield," Marcel had said. "He was protecting something—or someone."

Jean-Pierre closed his eyes, letting the words echo in his mind. He thought about the tools available to Louis during his time—limited technology, rudimentary communication methods, and a reliance on codes and cyphers to ensure messages could not be intercepted. The key had to be something simple yet effective.

His gaze fell on a weathered book on the corner of his desk: a French-English dictionary that had belonged to Louis. He pulled it towards him, flipping through the pages. An idea sparked.

"What if the code is tied to a language shift?" he muttered to himself. He quickly began scribbling notes, translating each letter of the code into corresponding numbers and pairing them with words in the dictionary. The process was laborious, but each small breakthrough filled him with renewed determination.

Hours passed, and the storm of papers on his desk grew. Finally, a pattern began to emerge. Certain letters matched specific pages and line numbers in the dictionary. Piece by piece, the cryptic message began to reveal itself.

Jean-Pierre leaned forward, his heart pounding as he decoded the final line. The message was simple, yet its implications were profound:

45.6789° N, 4.1234° E

Coordinates. The realisation hit him like a thunderclap. These numbers pointed to a location, and not just any location—a specific site tied to the French Resistance. Beneath the coordinates was a single phrase, written in French:

"Pour la liberté, nous combattons."

"For freedom, we fight," Jean-Pierre whispered, the words sending a chill down his spine. His grandfather had left behind a breadcrumb— a trace of a mission long buried in the annals of history. But what was the significance of this location? What had Louis Dupont been protecting?

The implications of the discovery hit Jean-Pierre hard. If these coordinates were tied to a Resistance mission, they might lead to hidden documents, artefacts, or even remnants of the war that could shed light on Louis's role. But with that realisation came a sense of urgency. The secrecy surrounding the message suggested that its contents might still be sensitive—or dangerous.

Jean-Pierre's thoughts raced. Who else might know about this? Could others be searching for the same answers? He glanced at the clock on the wall. It was nearly midnight, but sleep was the last thing on his mind. He grabbed his phone and dialled his father.

Marcel answered after a few rings, his voice groggy but alert. "Jean-Pierre? What is it?"

"I've cracked the code," Jean-Pierre said, barely able to contain his excitement. "They are coordinates, *Papa*. Coordinates tied to a mission from the Resistance. I think Louis left them as a clue."

Marcel was silent for a moment, the weight of the revelation sinking in. "Coordinates? Are you certain?"

"Yes. And there's a phrase too: 'For freedom, we fight.'"

Marcel exhaled slowly. "That… was his motto. He used to say it when I was a boy. Jean-Pierre, this is significant. But you must be cautious. Whatever Louis was protecting, he took great pains to keep hidden. There could be a reason for that."

"I know," Jean-Pierre said. "But I can't ignore this. I need to find out what's there."

"Very well," Marcel said after a pause. "But you won't go alone. Let me come with you. If this involves the Resistance, it's as much my legacy as it is yours."

Jean-Pierre agreed, feeling a mixture of relief and anticipation. They would go together, father and son, to uncover the secrets Louis Dupont had left behind.

***

The next morning, Jean-Pierre gathered Chantelle and Adrien to share the news. As they sat around the breakfast table, he laid out the coordinates and explained their significance. Ana, seated quietly beside him, listened with a mixture of curiosity and unease. Though she understood that this investigation was deeply personal—a Dupont matter—she couldn't help but feel a twinge of apprehension. Jean-Pierre had shared little with her about the details so far, and while she respected his need to unravel this mystery, she wished he would let her in more. Her gaze flickered between him and the coordinates, her hand resting on Pascal's shoulder as he played with a toy at her side.

Chantelle listened intently, her face showing full concentration. "This is extraordinary, Jean-Pierre. But it's also risky. If these coordinates are tied to a Resistance mission, there could be more to this than we realise. Have you considered what might happen if others find out about this?"

Adrien, ever the pragmatist, chimed in. "She's right. But this discovery is too important to ignore. If you're going to pursue this, you need to be prepared for what you might find—and for the possibility that it might not be what you expect."

Jean-Pierre nodded, appreciating their input. "I understand the risks. But this is our family's history. I can't turn away from it."

"Then let us help," Chantelle said firmly. "We'll support you, but we need to approach this carefully."

Together, the family began to plan their next steps. They researched the coordinates, discovering they pointed to a remote area in the French countryside, not far from where the Resistance had been active during the war. Jean-Pierre reached out to a historian specialising in the French Resistance, hoping to gather more context before making the journey.

Ana moved around the kitchen, preparing tea, her presence a quiet but grounding force amid the discussion.

Jean-Pierre had spoken to Ana the night before, sharing his discovery in a rushed, breathless recount. While she listened patiently, she couldn't help but feel a sense of distance—a chasm forming between them, not out of lack of love but from Jean-Pierre's singular focus on this investigation. She had nodded, encouraged him even, but deep down, she felt the faint stirrings of a question: where did she fit into all of this?

As the discussion ebbed, Ana remained quiet, her thoughts drifting elsewhere. Watching Jean-Pierre trace the lineage of his family, she couldn't help but wonder about her own roots. Her family had farmed this land for generations, their lives woven into the soil and the seasons. Were they just quiet witnesses to history, or had they played their own roles in the Resistance, unseen and unsung?

She thought of the old tales her grandmother used to tell—the hushed whispers about men disappearing into the woods at night, the coded messages passed through village hands, and the silent tension that had gripped the valley during the war. This land, their land, had seen more than its share of secrets.

Ana glanced at Jean-Pierre, so consumed by his quest, and felt a faint pang of envy. She longed to know more about her own heritage, but where would she even begin? And would the answers be as inspiring—or as haunting—as those Jean-Pierre was uncovering?

Her gaze shifted to Chantelle, who was cautioning Jean-Pierre about becoming too absorbed in the past, and Adrien, who balanced his encouragement with reminders of the family's present responsibilities. Ana smiled faintly, grateful for their voices and for the steadying effect they had on Jean-Pierre. Yet her reflections lingered as the conversation continued around her, quiet questions waiting for their moment to surface.

***

As the day wore on, Jean-Pierre found himself reflecting on the weight of his discovery. The coordinates represented more than just a location—they were a link to a past that had shaped his family's identity. He thought about Louis Dupont, a man who had risked everything for freedom, and wondered what secrets the journey would uncover.

That evening, as the family gathered for dinner, the mood was a mix of excitement and apprehension. Marcel shared stories of Louis's bravery, painting a picture of a man who had lived with unwavering principles and a deep sense of duty.

"Louis always said that freedom was worth any sacrifice," Marcel said, his voice tinged with emotion. "He believed in a better world, even when the odds were against him. If these coordinates lead to something he left behind, it's because he wanted us to find it. But we must tread carefully. The past has a way of reaching into the present in ways we don't always expect."

Jean-Pierre listened; his resolve strengthened. He didn't yet know what the journey would reveal, but he was ready to face it—not just for himself but for his family and for the legacy Louis Dupont had left behind.

Mario Zatta

Chapter 15

The morning air was crisp, carrying the faint scent of damp earth and ripening vines. Jean-Pierre stood at the edge of the vineyard, his gaze scanning the neat rows of grapevines that stretched towards the horizon. Adrien approached, his hands tucked into the pockets of his jacket, his presence unassuming yet reassuring. Despite being a doctor by profession, Adrien found solace in the physical labour of the vineyard during his time off. It was a stark contrast to the sterile halls of the hospital and a way to connect with Jean-Pierre and Chantelle.

"You're up early," Jean-Pierre remarked, his voice warm but tinged with the weight of unspoken thoughts.

"Chantelle mentioned you could use an extra pair of hands," Adrien replied. "Besides, it's nice to be out here. There's something grounding about working with the land."

Jean-Pierre nodded, appreciating Adrien's willingness to help. Despite Adrien's reserved nature, his bond with Jean-Pierre had deepened over the years, built on mutual respect and shared moments like these.

Together, they moved through the vineyard, inspecting the vines for signs of disease or damage. Jean-Pierre explained the nuances of viticulture, from understanding the soil to managing pests, his voice animated despite his usual reserved demeanour.

"You've got a knack for this," Adrien observed as he carefully pruned a vine under Jean-Pierre's guidance. "Do you ever miss being out here full-time, with all the other projects you're involving yourself with?"

Jean-Pierre hesitated, his hands stilling as he looked out over the vineyard. "Sometimes," he admitted. "But the winery isn't just about the land—it's about the legacy. That's what drives me now."

Adrien considered this, sensing the layers beneath Jean-Pierre's words. "Legacy is important," he said, "but don't forget the present. You've got a family who needs you here and now."

Jean-Pierre's lips curved into a faint smile. "You sound like Chantelle."

"She's a wise woman," Adrien replied with a grin.

The conversation flowed easily as they worked, their camaraderie evident in the comfortable silences and shared efforts. The vineyard, with its quiet beauty, became a backdrop for reflection and connection.

As the day wore on, their rhythm was interrupted by the arrival of two strangers. The men, dressed casually but with an air of practised ease, approached the edge of the vineyard, their movements purposeful. Jean-Pierre and Adrien exchanged a glance, their instincts sharpening.

"Can I help you?" Jean-Pierre called out; his tone polite but firm as he stepped forward.

One of the men, tall with a confident demeanour, offered a friendly smile. "We were just passing through and heard about the Dupont winery. Thought we'd stop by and learn a bit about its history."

Adrien's eyes narrowed slightly, his posture subtly shifting as he moved to stand beside Jean-Pierre. "The winery isn't open to visitors today," he said evenly. "But there's plenty of information available online if you're interested."

The second man, shorter but equally self-assured, chimed in. "We're more interested in the family history. The Dupont name carries a lot of weight in these parts."

Jean-Pierre's jaw tightened, though his expression remained composed. "Family history isn't something we discuss with strangers," he said, his voice firm.

The taller man raised his hands in a placating gesture. "Fair enough. No harm meant. We're just history enthusiasts, that's all."

Adrien stepped forward; his stance protective. "If that's the case, you'll understand why we value our privacy."

The men exchanged a look before nodding, their smiles faintly strained. "Of course," the shorter one said. "Thanks for your time."

As the strangers retreated, Adrien turned to Jean-Pierre. "That was odd."

Jean-Pierre nodded, his gaze following the men until they disappeared from view. "Too many questions for a casual visit."

"You think they're connected to what you've been digging into?" Adrien asked.

"Possibly," Jean-Pierre admitted. He paused as his mind flashed back to the car chase and the man who approached him in the village, and then continued, "But until we know more, we stay vigilant."

Adrien's expression darkened with concern. "You're not in this alone, Jean-Pierre. If there's something bigger at play, you've got people who've got your back."

Jean-Pierre met his gaze, gratitude flickering in his hazel eyes. "I appreciate that, Adrien. More than you know."

The rest of the day passed uneventfully, though the encounter lingered in their minds. As dusk settled over the vineyard, Jean-Pierre stood with Adrien, their bond strengthened by the day's events.

"Thanks for today," Jean-Pierre said, his voice quieter now. "For everything."

Adrien clapped a hand on his shoulder. "Anytime. We're family, Jean-Pierre. That means something."

Jean-Pierre nodded, the weight of his responsibilities feeling a little lighter. As they headed back towards the château, the vineyard bathed in the warm glow of the setting sun, he resolved to protect the legacy they were building—not just for the past, but for the future.

Chapter 16

The Dupont château glowed warmly against the encroaching night, its tall windows illuminated by soft light and laughter spilling out into the crisp evening air. Inside, the heart of the family pulsed with life and connection, and Friday night dinner promised the rare occasion where everyone gathered under one roof.

In the spacious kitchen, the air was thick with the rich aromas of roasted garlic, thyme, and freshly baked bread. Chantelle leaned against the counter, her arms crossed, a warm smile on her face as she chatted with Ana, who stood by the stove stirring a pot of creamy mushroom soup. Ana's movements were graceful and deliberate, her attention split between perfecting the dish and enjoying the conversation.

"Do you remember Giselle's reaction to the carrots last week?" Chantelle teased, watching Ana.

Ana chuckled, shaking her head. "How could I forget? She made it her mission to convince Pascal they were poisoned. I'm amazed she'll eat anything green at all."

The two women shared a laugh, their easy camaraderie reflecting the bond they'd built over the years. Chantelle reached for a bowl of salad and began tossing it, the clinking of utensils blending with the symphony of sizzling pans and bubbling pots.

In the adjoining dining room, Adrien stood beside Jean-Pierre, examining the rows of carefully labelled wine bottles in the vintage oak cabinet. The smell of aged wood and earthy notes of cork wafted as Adrien uncorked a bottle of Cabernet Franc.

"You've got an enviable collection," Adrien said, holding the bottle to the light. "Is this the one we're opening tonight?"

Jean-Pierre smirked. "That depends. Do you want to impress the ladies or make them laugh at how bad our taste is?"

Adrien grinned, shaking his head. "Definitely impress them. Let's go with this."

As Adrien placed the bottle on the counter, Jean-Pierre leaned closer, dropping his voice to a mock-serious tone. "You know, maybe you should think about ditching the hospital and coming to work in the vineyard. Here, the vines give back to you; they don't die on you."

Adrien burst into laughter, drawing Marcel's attention from across the room. Marcel, with Giselle perched on his lap, raised his glass and quipped, "Ah, but Adrien would miss all the drama of saving lives. Though vines *can* be just as dramatic, especially when they're stubborn."

Everyone laughed, the playful banter setting the tone for the evening. Pascal, giggling, scrambled onto Genevieve's lap and began animatedly describing his latest adventure in the vineyard—an exaggerated tale of chasing a rabbit that somehow turned into a dragon. Genevieve listened intently, her expression one of pure delight as she hung on his every word.

The family eventually settled around the long wooden dining table, the spread of dishes in front of them reflecting Ana's dedication and skill. As the glasses were poured and plates filled, the conversation meandered through everyday topics before settling, inevitably, on heritage and ancestry.

It was Adrien who first brought up the subject, leaning back in his chair. "So, Jean-Pierre, any new revelations about our mysterious Louis Dupont?"

Jean-Pierre, who had been slicing into a piece of roast chicken, paused. "Nothing concrete yet," he admitted. "But I have a feeling we're on the brink of something big. The connections keep leading back to the Resistance."

Ana leaned forward; her expression thoughtful. "You know, my family has been in this area for generations too. My grandparents never spoke much about the war, but I've always wondered. Maybe they were involved in some way, like Louis."

Jean-Pierre leaned back in his chair, his gaze drifting towards the crackling fireplace. Ana's words settled over him like a layer of mist, adding complexity to the narrative he'd been constructing in his mind. He had been so focused on his lineage, the coded letter, and Louis Dupont's heroism that he hadn't paused to consider the possibility that Ana's family—or even Adrien's—might have played a part in the same chapter of history. He studied Ana's face, illuminated by the flickering light, and felt a flicker of guilt. In his drive to uncover the past, he realised he might have overlooked the stories that had quietly existed alongside his own. The thought of their families being intertwined, united by something as monumental as the Resistance, added a weight he hadn't anticipated. "What if," he thought, "this isn't just my story to unravel, but ours?"

"It's possible," Adrien said, picking up the thread. "My grandfather used to tell me stories about people hiding in the mountains, smuggling messages and supplies. He never said outright that he was involved, but… who knows?"

Chantelle nodded, her face alight with curiosity. "It's fascinating to think how many untold stories there must be, especially in a region like this. People had to make impossible choices during that time."

Adrien, ever the pragmatist, grinned and teased Jean-Pierre. "Wouldn't it be something if all our grandparents worked together? Imagine, a secret team of local heroes, and here we are, their descendants, trying to piece it all together."

Jean-Pierre laughed, shaking his head. "You might be onto something, Adrien. Though, with all this talk of secret societies and hidden missions, it's starting to feel like a novel."

The table erupted in laughter, but Marcel's voice soon cut through, measured and reflective. "It's worth remembering that for our ancestors, these choices weren't made lightly. Louis Dupont's involvement in the Resistance was always shrouded in secrecy for a reason. It wasn't just about survival; it was about protecting others, even at great personal risk."

The room quieted as Marcel continued, his voice heavy with the weight of history. "The Resistance wasn't glamorous. It was dangerous and morally complex. Imagine having to decide whether to shelter someone, knowing it could mean your family's death. Or having to destroy a supply line, knowing it might harm innocent people down the chain. These weren't black-and-white decisions."

Jean-Pierre watched his father closely, absorbing the gravity of his words. "Do you think Louis ever doubted what he was doing?"

Marcel hesitated; his gaze distant as if searching through the past. "I don't know. But I'd like to believe he acted with a sense of justice, even when it wasn't easy. That's what we have to consider as we uncover these stories. They're not just history; they're reflections of the choices that define us."

Genevieve reached over to squeeze Marcel's hand, her eyes glistening. "And those choices remind us of who we are, where we come from. It's why this family—our traditions, our connections— matters so much."

As the dinner wound down, the conversation shifted to lighter topics, but the weight of Marcel's reflections lingered. For Jean-Pierre, the evening reinforced his determination to honour the past while safeguarding the present. And for Ana and Adrien, it was a reminder that the stories of their families—like the Duponts—might hold secrets yet to be uncovered.

When dessert was served and Giselle and Pascal began chasing each other around the room, laughter once again filled the air. Yet, for each member of the family, the night had stirred something deeper—a renewed sense of purpose, a connection to those who came before, and a bond that would carry them forward.

Mario Zatta

Chapter 17

The following morning, as the first light of dawn filtered through the grand windows of the château, Genevieve sat in her favourite armchair by the hearth. A steaming cup of tea rested in her hands, and her gaze lingered on the rolling vineyards outside. The landscape was tranquil, but her mind was anything but. Jean-Pierre's growing obsession with the coded letter, and now Ana's revelation, weighed heavily on her. She knew her son's determination was a double-edged sword—a trait he had undoubtedly inherited from both her and Marcel. Yet, as a mother, she couldn't shake the unease settling in her chest.

When Chantelle wandered in, still in her robe and cradling her cup of coffee, she found her mother deep in thought. "*Maman?*" she asked, her voice soft but concerned.

Genevieve glanced up and smiled faintly. "Good morning, *ma chère.*"

"You're up early," Chantelle observed, settling into the chair opposite her.

Genevieve nodded, her fingers curling tightly around her mug. "I couldn't sleep. Too much on my mind."

Chantelle tilted her head, waiting for her mother to continue. Genevieve sighed, her shoulders slumping slightly as if releasing a burden. "Do you remember the stories I used to tell you about my parents during the war?"

Chantelle nodded. "A little. I remember you saying they lived in constant fear, always looking over their shoulders."

Genevieve's eyes softened. "Yes. They did. My father was a schoolteacher, a quiet man, but when the war came, he became something else entirely. He joined a local Resistance cell, smuggling messages and supplies, hiding people who were fleeing. My mother… she was his anchor, much like I try to be for your father. She ran the household, kept us safe, and pretended we were just another ordinary family in a small town. But the strain… oh, Chantelle, the strain was unimaginable."

Her voice faltered, and Chantelle reached out, placing her hand over her mother's. "What happened?"

Genevieve swallowed hard, memories flooding back. "There was a raid one night. Someone had betrayed their cell. Soldiers came to our home, searching for my father. I'll never forget how my mother stood firm, staring them down while my father hid in a secret compartment under the floorboards. I thought my heart would stop beating that night."

Chantelle's eyes widened. "Did they find him?"

"No," Genevieve replied, her voice tinged with both relief and lingering fear. "But they left chaos in their wake—smashed furniture, torn books, a house that no longer felt like home. My parents never spoke of it afterwards, but I could see it in their eyes. They carried the weight of those nights for the rest of their lives."

She paused her gaze far away. "And now, Jean-Pierre is digging into the past, unearthing secrets that were meant to stay buried. I'm proud of his determination, but I'm also terrified, Chantelle. What if this investigation puts him—and all of us—in danger? What if the truths he uncovers hurt more than they heal?"

Chantelle leaned forward; her expression pensive. "Do you think he should stop?"

Genevieve hesitated, then shook her head. "No. He has a right to know. But I want him to tread carefully. The past is full of shadows, and not all of them are harmless. He needs to remember that he has a family here—a wife, children, a legacy of his own to protect."

The room fell silent for a moment, save for the crackling of the fire. Then Genevieve's tone softened. "I just wish I could shield him from the worst of it. But perhaps my role now is to remind him of the present, to keep him grounded in the love and life he has here."

Chantelle nodded, her admiration for her mother clear. "You've always been the glue that holds us together, *Maman.* Maybe Jean-Pierre needs that now more than ever."

Genevieve managed a small smile, though her heart remained heavy. She resolved to speak to Jean-Pierre later, to gently share her concerns and ensure that he approached his investigation with both courage and caution. She knew Marcel would support her, as he always had, but this time, the weight of keeping the family grounded seemed heavier than ever.

As the morning unfolded, Genevieve carried her memories like a fragile heirloom—both a warning and a testament to resilience. For the sake of her son, her family, and their future, she would do everything in her power to balance the scales of the past and the present.

Chapter 18

Jean-Pierre sat at the breakfast table, the morning sun streaming through the windows of the château, illuminating the polished wood and intricate patterns of the tablecloth. They all got together today for breakfast at the château, as Jean-Pierre knew his parents loved seeing their grandchildren. Across from Jean-Pierre, Ana poured milk into Giselle's cereal while Pascal, as usual, was more interested in using his spoon as a catapult than eating.

"I've been thinking," Jean-Pierre began, glancing at Marcel and Genevieve, who were sipping their coffee. "We could all use a break. I would like to go to Saint Etienne for a day. It's been a tense few weeks, and I thought maybe we could take a trip—to Annecy, on the way to Saint-Étienne. Let's have a break, and spend some time together."

Genevieve looked up, her eyes softening. "Annecy? Oh Jean-Pierre, I love Annecy."

"Yes," Jean-Pierre said. "It's on the route, Ana. A beautiful town by a lake, with canals, history, and charm. I thought it might do us some good to get away for a couple of days; enjoy ourselves."

Ana raised an eyebrow, her scepticism evident. "Are you sure this is about relaxing and not just an excuse to keep digging into your family history?"

Jean-Pierre reached for her hand. "This is for you, Ana. For the kids, for my parents. You've all been so patient with me. I want us to enjoy something together—no research, no stress."

Ana studied him for a moment before nodding. "Okay, but only if you promise: no sneaking off to ask questions."

Jean-Pierre smiled. "I do want to visit the museum and the monuments in Saint Etienne, but that is it. Promise. The rest of the time is for all of us to enjoy. Promise"

***

The family left early the next morning, the Range Rover packed with overnight bags and picnic essentials. As the road curved through the mountains and valleys, they marvelled at the changing landscape.

"Look, *Maman*! Look, Mamie!" Giselle exclaimed, pointing out the window. "The mountains are so big!"

Genevieve smiled; her own gaze drawn to the snow-capped peaks. "Yes, darling. They remind me of when your grandfather and I first came here, years ago."

Ana turned her head and smiled at Giselle, nodding in agreement.

The drive took them through breathtaking scenery that unfolded like a living postcard, each mile revealing a new masterpiece of nature and tradition. Rolling fields of vibrant green stretched to the horizon, speckled with bursts of wildflowers in yellows, purples, and reds, their colours vivid against the backdrop of the towering French Alps. Villages dotted the valleys, their typical wooden Swiss chalets standing proudly with steep, sloping roofs and intricately carved balconies adorned with cascading geraniums in full bloom. Smoke spiralled lazily from the chimneys, suggesting the warmth of roaring fireplaces inside.

The winding road followed the curves of a glistening stream, its waters so clear that the polished stones at the bottom sparkled like jewels under the golden sunlight. Forests of towering pines and firs blanketed the mountainsides, their needles releasing a fresh, earthy aroma that mingled with the faint, sweet scent of wildflowers carried by the breeze.

As they ascended gentle inclines, the air grew cooler and crisper, invigorating with every breath. In the fields, herds of brown-and-white cows grazed lazily, their bells creating a gentle, melodic clinking that complemented the natural symphony of birdsong and the distant rush of waterfalls tumbling down rocky cliffs.

Jean-Pierre slowed the car as they passed through a quaint hamlet, where timber-framed houses with brightly painted shutters seemed to smile beneath the embrace of blooming window boxes. Locals waved warmly, their pace unhurried, as if time moved more slowly in this idyllic corner of the world.

The weather was perfect—blue skies stretched endlessly above, broken only by fluffy clouds that cast playful shadows over the patchwork of meadows and forests below. The golden sunlight filtered through the trees, creating dappled patterns on the road and illuminating the landscape in hues that seemed almost too vivid to be real.

The scent of freshly cut hay mixed with the faint aroma of wood smoke and damp earth as the family rolled down their windows to take it all in. Streams shimmered like ribbons of silver, their babbling chorus providing a soothing backdrop to their journey. Every bend in the road revealed another breathtaking tableau, whether it was a rustic bridge spanning a gurgling brook or a panoramic view of the snow-capped peaks towering above.

By the time they descended into the valley leading to Annecy, the scenery had painted a storybook journey that would forever linger in their memories. But nothing quite prepared them for the sight of Annecy itself, nestled along the sparkling lake with its medieval charm and Alpine grace, as if it had been placed there by the hands of an artist.

 Known as the *Venice of the Alps,* the town greeted them with its turquoise lake reflecting the surrounding mountains and its charming canals crisscrossing the old town.

***

After checking into a quaint boutique hotel overlooking the lake, the family set out to explore Annecy. The cobblestone streets of the old town were lined with pastel-coloured houses adorned with flower boxes spilling over with geraniums. Cafés and restaurants stretched along the canals; their outdoor seating filled with people enjoying the late afternoon sun.

"What's that smell?" Pascal said, his nose twitching.

"Crêpes," Marcel said with a grin, pointing to a nearby stall where a vendor was expertly flipping thin pancakes.

The family stopped to share a freshly made crêpe dusted with sugar, the warm, buttery treat melting in their mouths.

As they wandered further, they came to the Palais de l'Isle, a medieval castle nestled like a jewel in the heart of the canal. Originally built in the 12th century, it had served many purposes over the centuries: a residence for the local lord, a courthouse, and even a prison. Its walls, weathered by time, bore silent witness to Annecy's history, from the Middle Ages to the Renaissance and beyond. The castle's unique triangular design gave it the appearance of a ship moored in the water, earning it the nickname *"the old prison."* Today, it stands as both a museum and a monument, a reminder of the city's layered past.

The family paused on the bridge overlooking the Palais, marvelling at its timeless grandeur. Below them, the canal split at the castle's triangular corner, flowing in two directions like twin veins of the city's lifeblood. The gentle current rippled softly against the stone foundations, catching the late afternoon sunlight in shimmering reflections.

Flower boxes lined the edges of the canal, brimming with vibrant blooms of geraniums, petunias, and begonias. Their brilliant reds, pinks, and purples contrasted beautifully with the earthy stone of the old buildings and the clear blue sky above. The air was fragrant with the soft, sweet scent of flowers, mingled with the faint aroma of fresh bread and pastries wafting from nearby cafes.

Giselle leaned over the railing, her eyes wide with wonder. "It looks like a castle from a fairy tale," she said, her voice filled with awe.

"It does, doesn't it?" Genevieve replied, her gaze lingering on the castle. "And to think, it's stood here for almost a thousand years, watching over Annecy through wars and peace."

Jean-Pierre lifted Pascal onto his shoulders so he could get a better view. The little boy giggled as he pointed at the flower boxes. "So many flowers, *Papa*!"

Ana, standing beside Jean-Pierre, took his hand and squeezed it. "It's beautiful," she said softly, her eyes moving between the castle and the canals.

Marcel rested his hands on the bridge's railing, his expression thoughtful. "It's remarkable," he said, his deep voice tinged with admiration. "Imagine the stories these walls could tell if they could speak."

The family lingered for a moment, soaking in the scene: the stillness of the canal, the rustle of the flower petals in the breeze, and the muted chatter of passersby strolling along the water's edge. It was as if time had paused, allowing them to stand between history and the present, united as a family in the shadow of Annecy's iconic landmark.

"This place feels like a fairytale," Ana said, taking Giselle's hand as they moved off the small bridge.

"During the war, Annecy wasn't just beautiful; it was significant," Marcel said, his voice thoughtful. "The Resistance operated in this region, using the mountains and the lake for strategic movements."

"Really?" Jean-Pierre asked, intrigued.

"Yes," Marcel continued. "Annecy was a refuge for many, but it also saw its share of sorrow. People were smuggled to safety here, but others were captured and sent to camps. The town carries both beauty and a heavy history."

The family continued their walk through the *Jardins de l'Europe,* a lush park on the edge of the lake. Towering trees lined the paths, their leaves rustling softly in the breeze. Giselle and Pascal ran ahead, chasing each other around the fountains and statues that dotted the park.

"This is exactly what we needed," Ana said, leaning into Jean-Pierre as they walked. "Thank you for bringing us here."

Jean-Pierre squeezed her hand. "It's good to see you smile again."

As they continued their stroll, Jean-Pierre gently guided Ana towards the *Pont des Amours,* the "Bridge of Love," which arched gracefully over the canal connecting the *Jardins de l'Europe* to the lakefront. The bridge, with its ornate iron railings, was a favourite spot for couples and carried a legend that had endured for generations.

"Do you know the story of this bridge?" Jean-Pierre asked as they paused at the centre, the water below shimmering in the golden light of sunset.
Ana shook her head, her eyes curious.
"They say that whoever you kiss on this bridge will be yours forever," Jean-Pierre said, his voice soft as he leaned closer. He tilted her chin gently towards him and pressed a tender kiss to her lips, the world around them momentarily fading.

Nearby, Genevieve and Marcel stood side by side, watching the younger couple with fond smiles. Marcel reached for Genevieve's hand, lacing his fingers through hers. "What do you think?" he asked, his voice warm with nostalgia.

Genevieve turned to him, her green eyes twinkling. "I think it's a beautiful story."

Marcel smiled and bent slightly, brushing his lips against hers. For a moment, it was as though time had rolled back, and they were once again the young couple who had shared their first adventures together.

Around them, the breeze carried the laughter of their grandchildren, and the soft murmur of water beneath the bridge underscored the quiet intimacy of the moment. It was a rare instance of tranquillity, a memory they would all treasure in the days to come.

The park opened up to the lakefront, where sailboats bobbed gently in the water. The mountains loomed in the background, their reflection shimmering on the lake's surface.

That afternoon, they rented a small boat and set out onto the lake. Jean-Pierre took the wheel, guiding them across the calm waters. The children leaned over the sides, Ana holding on tightly to Pascal, their laughter echoing across the lake as they trailed their fingers in the water.

"This lake is one of the purest in Europe," Marcel said, his voice filled with admiration. "Glacial waters feed it, and the surrounding environment is carefully protected."

Genevieve, sitting beside him, nodded. "It's incredible. So much history here, too. And like your father said, it was a centre for resistance fighters during the war?"

"I've read bits and pieces about Saint Etienne and surrounding areas," Jean-Pierre admitted. "I had no idea this had history too. And it is just so beautiful."

The family paused for a moment to take in the beauty of the small tree-laden island in the middle of the lake set against the backdrop of the French Alps. They fell silent as the boat drifted, and the more they looked around, the more they appreciated the serene beauty of their surroundings.

***

That evening, they dined at a cosy restaurant tucked into one of the old town's narrow streets. The air was filled with the rich aroma of melted cheese and fresh bread, drawing them inside.

They ordered a traditional Savoyard cheese fondue, which arrived at the table bubbling in a heavy cast-iron pot. Long forks were provided, and the family took turns dipping chunks of crusty bread into the molten cheese. A children-friendly version with milder cheese, milk and cream was prepared for the children so that they could enjoy the experience of dipping bread. Giselle kept losing hers while Pascal was happy to sit on Ana's lap and let her feed him.

"This is delicious!" Giselle declared, her cheeks pink with excitement, losing yet another morsel of bread.

"Don't forget the wine, Jean-Pierre" Marcel said, pouring glasses of a crisp, local white wine for the adults. "A meal like this isn't complete without it."

Jean-Pierre chuckled as he leaned back in his chair. "A good meal isn't complete without the pudding," he replied with a playful grin, glancing at Giselle and Pascal. Their faces lit up, eyes wide with anticipation, as they turned their attention to the dessert menu displayed on a small chalkboard at the corner of the restaurant.

Soon, the table was filled with a spread of traditional Savoyard pastries and desserts, each one more enticing than the last. There was *tarte aux myrtilles*, a rustic blueberry tart made with wild berries from the nearby Alps, its glossy, dark filling glistening under the soft lights. Plates of *bugnes*, crisp and delicate fried pastries dusted generously with powdered sugar, sat beside bowls of *crème brûlée,* their caramelised tops cracking satisfyingly under the tap of a spoon to reveal velvety custard beneath.

A *gâteau de Savoie*, a light sponge cake with hints of lemon and dusted with confectioners' sugar, stood as a centrepiece, its simple elegance reminiscent of the region's alpine charm. For the chocolate lovers, there was *fondant au chocolat*, a decadent molten lava cake served warm, its gooey centre oozing onto plates with each bite.

Giselle and Pascal dove in with unrestrained delight. Giselle's lips turned purple as she devoured slice after slice of the *tarte aux myrtilles*, her cheeks puffed like a squirrel's as she savoured the tangy sweetness of the berries. Pascal, meanwhile, found himself enchanted by the *bugnes,* laughing as powdered sugar coated his tiny hands and face with each bite.

Jean-Pierre reached over, grabbing a piece of the *gâteau de Savoie.* "Careful, Pascal, you're wearing more sugar than you're eating," he teased, earning a burst of giggles from both children.

Ana smiled warmly, watching the scene unfold. She leaned towards Jean-Pierre, her voice low but playful. "If you behave yourself, Jean-Pierre, I might make you one of these at home," she teased, motioning towards the *tarte aux myrtilles*.

Jean-Pierre raised his eyebrows in mock surprise. "That might be the best reason I've ever had to behave," he said, his grin widening.

Even Marcel and Genevieve indulged, savouring the local delicacies as they traded stories from the past. Genevieve reminisced about learning to make *crème brûlée* during her youth, sharing tips with Ana as the two women discussed the desserts with the air of connoisseurs.

The evening stretched on, filled with the sound of laughter, the clinking of glasses, and the delighted squeals of the children. Around the table, under the glow of the restaurant's warm lanterns and surrounded by the timeless beauty of Annecy, the Dupont family found a moment of pure joy—a feast for both the palate and the soul.

The conversation flowed so easily, and the laughter replaced the tension that had hung over them for weeks. For the first time in what felt like ages, Jean-Pierre felt a sense of peace.

***

Later that night, Jean-Pierre and Ana sat on the balcony of their hotel room, looking out over the twinkling lights of Annecy reflected on the lake.

"Thank you for this," Ana said, resting her head on his shoulder. "It's been a while since we've had a moment like this."

Jean-Pierre kissed her hair. "You and the kids deserve it. I know I've been... distracted lately."

Ana looked up at him, her expression serious. "Just promise me, Jean-Pierre, that whatever you find in this investigation won't tear us apart. The past is the past for a reason."

Jean-Pierre nodded, though he couldn't shake the feeling that the past wasn't quite finished with them yet.

For now, though, he let himself savour the quiet moments with his family, the beauty of Annecy, and the warmth of Ana by his side. Tomorrow would bring new challenges, but tonight, he allowed himself to simply be.

Chapter 19

The road from Annecy to Saint-Étienne stretched ahead, winding through some of the most picturesque landscapes France had to offer. The Dupont family set out early, the morning sun casting long, vibrant rays over the rolling hills and valleys. The drive was serene, a perfect continuation of their time in Annecy, and Jean-Pierre took care to ensure the journey itself felt like an extension of their holiday.

As they left Annecy, the towering French Alps slowly gave way to gentler, forested hills. Quaint villages dotted the route, their stone cottages and red-tiled roofs framed by lush greenery. The fields were alive with colour—vivid greens of young grass and soft yellows of flowering rapeseed swaying gently in the breeze. In some places, small vineyards clung to the hillsides, their neat rows a testament to the region's agricultural traditions.

The family passed through valleys flanked by thick woodlands, where the trees—barely touched by the early frost—displayed hues of deep green and earthy brown. Streams glistened as they wound through the landscape, their clear waters reflecting the sunlight in dazzling bursts. Occasionally, a wooden bridge would appear, arching gracefully over the water and providing a fleeting glimpse of a fisherman casting his line or a family of ducks paddling downstream.

The architecture of the villages shifted subtly as they moved closer to Saint-Étienne. The traditional wooden Alpine, Savoyard chalets of Annecy gave way to more austere, practical designs—stone houses with slate roofs that seemed to belong to a region more attuned to industry than tourism. Church spires rose sharply against the horizon, marking the centres of small communities, while rustic barns and crumbling stone walls hinted at generations of farmers who had worked the land.

The weather, too, seemed to reflect the transition. Where Annecy had been bright and sunlit, the sky over the approach to Saint-Étienne was a softer blue, with a few scattered clouds. The air was crisp, carrying the faint scent of earth and woodsmoke from nearby farmhouses.

Saint-Étienne itself lay nestled among low hills, its modest skyline marked by a blend of old and new. Once a thriving hub of the French Industrial Revolution, the city carried a quiet dignity, its history woven into the fabric of its streets and buildings.

The Dupont family parked their car and stepped onto cobbled streets that seemed to whisper of a bygone era. Narrow lanes, lined with centuries-old stone buildings, curved between larger boulevards where grand 19th-century façades spoke of a time when the city was at the forefront of mining and metallurgy. The architecture was functional but elegant, with wrought iron balconies and large arched windows lending a touch of charm to the otherwise austere surroundings.

Genevieve pointed to a small square dominated by a weathered bronze statue of a miner holding a lantern. "That must be a tribute to their mining past," she mused.

Marcel nodded. "Saint-Étienne was a major coal and steel hub during the 19th and early 20th centuries. They even called it the 'City of Arms' for its weapon production."

As they walked, the city revealed its layers of history. Older sections bore the hallmarks of medieval architecture—churches with soaring Gothic spires, narrow alleyways that once bustled with market traders, and remnants of old city walls hidden between modern structures. The Basilica of Saint-Denis, with its ornate carvings and stained-glass windows, stood as a testament to the city's religious heritage.

In contrast, the newer parts of Saint-Étienne displayed their adaptability in the face of industrial decline. Public spaces were adorned with modern sculptures, and pedestrian-friendly zones bustled with cafes and boutiques. Murals depicting the city's history and culture brought splashes of colour to otherwise neutral facades.

Marcel paused outside a small museum, reading the plaque by its entrance. "This area was central to the production of ribbons," he said, gesturing towards the building. "Saint-Étienne was famous for them long before its rise in mining and metallurgy."

Genevieve smiled, taking in the blend of artistry and industry. "Ribbons, coal, weapons… It's fascinating how diverse the city's history is."

Saint-Étienne's industrial roots were everywhere, from the preserved mining equipment displayed in public squares to the repurposed factories that now housed art galleries and innovation centres. The city had embraced its past while striving towards reinvention, a duality that resonated deeply with the Dupont family as they walked its streets.

The family stopped at a local bakery for a late lunch, the smell of freshly baked bread and pastries filling the air. Giselle and Pascal eagerly pressed their noses against the glass display, pointing out their favourite treats.

"*Pain de seigle*," Ana said, holding up a slice of dense rye bread. "Perfect with cheese and honey."

"And don't forget the *tarte aux pommes*," Marcel added, indulging in the flaky, caramelised pastry.

The day passed quickly as they explored the city, enjoying its mix of historical landmarks and modern culture. Saint-Étienne had a quieter charm than Annecy, but its depth and character left an equally lasting impression.

As the sun began to set, casting an ethereal glow over the city, Jean-Pierre glanced at his family, their faces alight with curiosity and contentment. This journey, like their time in Annecy, was about more than uncovering history. It was about finding moments of connection, joy, and strength—qualities that had always defined the Dupont family.

* * *

The air in Saint-Étienne carried the weight of its history—heavy, solemn, yet brimming with a quiet pride. Jean-Pierre woke early that morning, feeling a sense of purpose he hadn't quite experienced before. The day's plan was his alone. While Marcel, Genevieve, Ana and the children enjoyed a quiet stroll through the old squares of the city interspersed with keeping Giselle and Pascal entertained at a local park, Jean-Pierre set out on foot, determined to explore the monuments and museums dedicated to the French Resistance.

As he moved through the narrow streets, the hum of morning life surrounded him—café doors clinked open, shopkeepers arranged displays of fresh baguettes, and the scent of roasting coffee beans drifted into the cool air. For all its modern activity, Jean-Pierre could feel something else beneath the surface: a pulse of the past. The same streets that bustled with everyday life now had once borne the silent footsteps of brave men and women.

His first destination was the Memorial to the Resistance and Deportation in Loire. Located in a discreet building that seemed unassuming at first, its quiet presence demanded reverence. Jean-Pierre entered through tall glass doors, and the modern design gave way to an interior steeped in memory.

The silence inside was thick, broken only by the faint echoes of footsteps on polished floors. Along the walls stretched haunting black-and-white photographs—faces of ordinary citizens who had become extraordinary fighters. Young men with determined gazes. Women, heads held high, their resolve unshaken. Families torn apart.

Jean-Pierre walked slowly, taking in each story, each exhibit. A detailed map outlined the industrial significance of Saint-Étienne during the German occupation, marking factories and railways that had become targets. He stopped at a display dedicated to the May 26, 1944, bombing, which described how the 15th U.S. Army Air Force targeted the city's armament production and railway installations.

The photographs were chilling. Entire blocks were reduced to rubble. Smoke billowing into the sky. Descriptions detailed the loss of civilian lives caught in the crossfire of liberation—a cruel price paid for freedom. Jean-Pierre's throat tightened as he imagined the chaos, the confusion. The realisation struck him that for so many residents, survival had not only meant enduring the occupation but enduring liberation itself.

Moving further into the exhibition, Jean-Pierre stopped at a section dedicated to the *Armée Secrète*, the clandestine organisation that played such a vital role in Saint-Étienne. Archival documents detailed its operations—sabotage missions, intelligence gathering, and daring raids to disrupt German supply lines.

One exhibit, surrounded by dim lighting, held particular gravity. A small display case contained artefacts belonging to local Resistance leaders—handwritten notes, weapons, and photographs. Jean-Pierre leaned closer and read the plaque:

"In early 1943, tragedy struck Saint-Étienne's Resistance. Key leaders of the Armée Secrète were arrested, leaving the network weakened but not broken. Despite the risks, local fighters continued their mission, preparing for the liberation."

The accompanying photograph was striking—four men, bound and blindfolded, being marched away by Nazi soldiers. Jean-Pierre couldn't tear his eyes away.

"Powerful, isn't it?"

Jean-Pierre turned, startled. An elderly man in a charcoal wool coat stood beside him, hands resting on a cane. His face was lined with age, his gaze soft but piercing.

"Yes," Jean-Pierre replied after a moment. "It's almost overwhelming."

The old man gave a small nod. "They paid dearly, those brave souls. Some were never seen again." He paused, his eyes scanning the photographs. "What brings you here, young man? Family history?"

Jean-Pierre hesitated, caught off guard. "In a way. I'm searching for details about my ancestor, Louis Dupont. I've recently learned he was part of the French Resistance, and his story brought me here."

The man's face shifted, a flicker of recognition passing across his features before he schooled it into neutrality. "Louis Dupont…" He murmured the name as if tasting it, weighing its significance. "He was one of the silent ones."

Jean-Pierre's pulse quickened. "You knew of him?"

"Not directly, no. But there were many like him—fighters who didn't seek glory. The kind who would rather fade into history than stand in its light." He paused. "Some names surface only when they need to be heard."

Jean-Pierre nodded, struck by the weight of the man's words. Before he could respond, the old man's gaze turned sharp. "Be careful, son. Stirring old ghosts doesn't always bring peace."

A chill ran down Jean-Pierre's spine. "What do you mean?"

The old man shrugged, his cane tapping against the floor as he turned away. "History has teeth."

***

Jean-Pierre emerged from the memorial, blinking against the afternoon sunlight. He carried the old man's words with him, their cryptic edge clinging to his thoughts.

His next stop was a short walk away: a monument in one of Saint-Étienne's older squares. *The Monument to the Fallen Resistance Fighters* stood tall and solemn, its stone etched with the names of local heroes. Fresh flowers had been placed at its base—a reminder that, even now, the sacrifices made so many years ago were not forgotten.

Jean-Pierre lingered, his eyes scanning the engraved names, wondering if Louis Dupont's name might appear. When he didn't find it, a small pang of disappointment surfaced, but he pushed it aside. Louis's heroism, it seemed, was not one for public memorials.

As he continued through the city, Jean-Pierre noticed the traces of its wartime scars. The industrial buildings that had once been targets of bombings still stood, some rebuilt and modernised, others left as silent testaments to what had occurred. The railway station—a focal point of Allied disruption—was now bustling with trains coming and going, its historic significance buried beneath the hum of modern life.

Jean-Pierre stopped for a coffee at a small café tucked into a corner near the station. As he sat beneath the striped awning, sipping his espresso, he overheard snippets of conversation in soft French. An older couple beside him spoke of *les années noires*—the "dark years" of the occupation—as if they were recounting a distant nightmare.

Jean-Pierre's thoughts drifted to Louis once more. He imagined his ancestor navigating these very streets under the cover of night, dodging patrols, meeting contacts in hidden corners, and risking everything to pass on intelligence or sabotage German efforts.

The stories of bravery that Jean-Pierre had read about in the memorial suddenly felt closer, more intimate. His ancestor had been one of those unsung heroes who'd quietly reshaped the course of history.

***

By evening, Jean-Pierre returned to the hotel where the family was staying. The lobby was warm and inviting, with its wood-panelled walls and faint aroma of fresh pastries. Marcel sat by the fireplace, a book in hand, while Genevieve played a game of cards with Giselle and Pascal on a nearby couch.

Ana was curled up in an armchair, looking out the window at the city's twinkling lights. She turned when she heard Jean-Pierre enter, her expression soft but searching.

"You were gone a while," she said quietly as he approached.

Jean-Pierre dropped into the seat beside her, letting out a slow breath. "There's so much history here. So much… pain and sacrifice."

Ana rested a hand on his arm. "Did you find what you were looking for?"

"Not yet. But I'm starting to see how big this all is—how much people fought, struggled, and suffered for the freedom we have now. It's humbling."

She gave him a small smile, but her eyes clouded with worry. "Just… don't lose yourself in it, Jean-Pierre. I know you're searching for answers, but you promised me the family wouldn't get hurt."

Jean-Pierre took her hand, squeezing it gently. "I won't let that happen."

Pascal suddenly bounded over, his face lit up with excitement. "*Papa*! We finished our game! I won!"

Jean-Pierre grinned, scooping his son into his lap. "Is that so? You must be a card-playing master!"

Giselle came trotting behind, her arms folded. "He cheated."

Genevieve's laughter rang out. "Now, now, cheating is just a creative strategy."

As the room filled with their laughter, Jean-Pierre felt grounded again—anchored by his family. The shadows of the past still lingered in his mind, but for now, he let the warmth of the present hold him steady. When they got back home, he would continue his search. For now, he would simply be a husband, a son, and a father.

Jean-Pierre stood by the window; his silhouette outlined by the faint glow of Saint-Étienne's city lights. The night outside was still, the streets quiet save for the occasional sound of a distant car or the soft chatter of late-night walkers. From his vantage point, he could see the city sprawled out before him, its mix of old stone buildings and modern structures whispering stories of resilience and change.

He slipped his hand into his pocket, his fingers brushing against the edges of the small flyer he'd taken from the memorial earlier that day. He pulled it out and unfolded it, smoothing the creases as his eyes settled on the emblem printed in faded ink—a symbol of the Resistance. Its bold, simple design spoke of defiance and unity, yet now, under the dim light of his bedside lamp, it seemed to carry an unspoken weight.

Jean-Pierre's mind wandered back to the old man at the memorial. His words had been enigmatic, but they lingered like smoke after a fire.

"History has teeth."

What had he meant? Was it a warning? A reflection? Or simply the musings of someone who had seen too much? Jean-Pierre wasn't sure, but the phrase gnawed at him, refusing to be ignored.

He gazed out at the city again, his thoughts drifting to the stories he'd encountered that day. The faces of resistance fighters stared back at him in his memory—brave, determined, and burdened by the weight of their choices. He thought of Louis Dupont, his elusive ancestor, and wondered if the man had stood in similar silence on nights like this, looking out over the same city, wrestling with the moral complexity of his actions.

The faint hum of voices from the next room reminded Jean-Pierre of his family. Giselle and Pascal had fallen asleep hours ago, their laughter now replaced by the soft rhythm of their breathing. Ana was tidying up their things for the next day, her movements calm and deliberate. Marcel and Genevieve were sharing a quiet conversation, their voices low and soothing.

For a moment, Jean-Pierre felt a pang of guilt. He was here with his family, surrounded by warmth and love, yet his thoughts seemed tethered to shadows of the past.

He folded the flyer carefully, as if afraid to damage its fragile connection to history and slipped it back into his pocket. But the unease remained; a subtle weight pressing against his chest. It wasn't fear exactly, but rather a growing awareness that the past he was uncovering might demand something of him—something he wasn't yet sure he could give.

Jean-Pierre closed his eyes briefly, taking a deep breath. When he opened them, he found himself looking at his faint reflection in the glass, superimposed over the city lights. He saw not just himself but also the echoes of those who had come before—fighters, survivors, and perhaps, ghosts.

The city seemed to hold its breath as if waiting for him to decide something he couldn't yet name.

With a soft sigh, Jean-Pierre turned away from the window, the flyer still tucked in his pocket. As he climbed into bed beside Ana, he glanced one last time at the city outside. The lights shimmered like stars, but beneath their glow, the shadows of history lingered, silent and watchful.

And somewhere, deep in his chest, that seed of unease began to sprout, its roots tangling with questions he wasn't sure he was ready to answer.

Chapter 20

The gravel crunched beneath the car tyres as the family pulled into the driveway of the Dupont château. The familiar sight of the stone estate, its ivy-covered façade bathed in the warm glow of the evening sun, brought a sense of comfort to everyone in the car. The door to the château swung open, and Chantelle stepped out onto the porch, her arms wide open. Adrien followed; a kitchen towel slung over his shoulder, offering a warm wave.

The car doors burst open as Giselle and Pascal scrambled out, their little legs propelling them towards Chantelle with delighted squeals of, "*Tata* Chantelle!" Aunty Chantelle knelt down just in time to catch the pair in a whirlwind of hugs and kisses.

"You won't believe what we saw!" Giselle exclaimed, her words tumbling out as Pascal eagerly chimed in, "And we went on a boat!"

"Slow down, you two!" Chantelle laughed, scooping Pascal into her arms while holding Giselle's hand. "Tell me everything during dinner. Adrien and I have something special waiting for you all."

Jean-Pierre helped Ana out of the car while Marcel and Genevieve gathered their things. The scent of freshly baked bread and savoury herbs wafted through the open windows, mingling with the crisp evening air. "That smells incredible," Genevieve remarked as she approached the house, her face lighting up at the prospect of a home-cooked meal after their journey.

Inside, the dining room table was set beautifully, a hearty meal steaming in serving dishes at its centre. Adrien stepped forward, beaming. "Welcome back! We thought we'd treat you all tonight." Chantelle added, "Adrien did most of the cooking, but I'll take credit for the dessert."
The family settled around the table, laughter and conversation flowing easily as plates were filled and wine was poured.

"This trip was exactly what we needed," Ana began, her voice warm as she looked at her husband. "Being together, seeing such beautiful places... it felt like a dream."

"It truly was," Genevieve agreed. "Annecy was my favourite. The canals, the food, the atmosphere—it's like stepping into another world."

Marcel nodded, raising his glass. "And let's not forget the wine. That crisp white from Annecy... it was something special."

As the adults reminisced, Giselle piped up, "And the ducks! Remember the ducks, Pascal?"

"And the boat ride!" Pascal added enthusiastically, his face lighting up at the memory.

The adults laughed, delighting in the children's excitement. Chantelle, who had been listening attentively, turned her gaze towards her brother. "And what about you, Jean-Pierre?"

Jean-Pierre smiled, setting his glass down. "For me, it was the landscape—those rolling hills, the fields, the Alps in the distance. And most of all, being with all of you. There's nothing better than that."

He paused, his expression growing more animated as he continued. "But I have to say, my day in Saint-Étienne left a deep impression. The museum, the monuments… they brought so much of our history to life. Seeing how people like Louis Dupont risked everything made me feel more connected to our past—and more inspired to understand it fully. It was a powerful experience."

Chantelle studied him for a moment, her expression thoughtful. "I admire your dedication, Jean-Pierre," she said softly, "but don't lose sight of what's right in front of you." Her gaze flicked briefly to Ana and the children.

Jean-Pierre nodded; his smile tinged with gratitude. "I won't. I promise."

The conversation picked up again, everyone talking at once—sharing jokes, recounting memories, and teasing each other. The warmth of the room, the clinking of glasses, and the sounds of happy voices filled the château, wrapping the family in a cocoon of togetherness.

***

Later, as the plates were cleared and dessert was being prepared in the kitchen, Ana lingered by the counter, watching Chantelle assemble the finishing touches on a fruit tart.

"Chantelle," Ana began hesitantly, her voice low, "can I talk to you for a moment?"

"Of course," Chantelle replied, glancing up with a reassuring smile.

Ana exhaled softly, her hands fidgeting with the edge of a dish towel. "I'm worried about Jean-Pierre. He's so consumed by this investigation. I know it's important to him, but… I can't shake the feeling that it's pulling him away—from us, from the kids. I think he might not be telling us everything and I worry. And with everything he's learning, I'm afraid it's only going to get worse."

Chantelle set the tart down and moved closer, placing a comforting hand on Ana's arm. "He's passionate about it, and sometimes that passion can feel overwhelming. But Jean-Pierre loves you and the kids. You're his anchor, Ana."

Adrien entered the kitchen just then, catching the tail end of their conversation. "What's going on?" he asked, a concerned look on his face.

Ana hesitated, but Chantelle answered for her. "Ana's worried about Jean-Pierre, about how much this investigation is consuming him."

Adrien leaned against the counter; his arms crossed. "Jean-Pierre's always been intense when he sets his mind to something. But he's also a good man. I'll talk to him and see if I can help him find some balance."

Ana smiled weakly; her gratitude clear. "Thank you, Adrien."

***

Later that night, after the children were tucked into bed and the adults were unwinding with glasses of wine, Adrien found an opportunity to pull Jean-Pierre aside. The two men stepped out onto the terrace, the cool night air carrying the faint scent of lavender from the garden.

"What's on your mind, Adrien?" Jean-Pierre asked, leaning on the railing and looking out at the darkened vineyard.

Adrien took a sip of his wine before answering. "You, actually. Ana's worried about you, and to be honest, so am I."

Jean-Pierre frowned, turning to face him. "Worried? About what?"

Adrien met his gaze evenly. "This investigation of yours. It's important, I get that. But it's also consuming you. Ana's afraid it's pulling you away from the family."

Jean-Pierre's shoulders tensed, but Adrien pressed on. "Look, you're chasing history, and I respect that. But don't forget to live in the present. Don't let the past rob you of the life you've built here—the life you're building with Ana and the kids."

Jean-Pierre looked down at his glass, his expression conflicted. "I'm not trying to neglect them. I'm doing this for all of us—for our legacy."

"And that's noble," Adrien said. "But legacy means nothing if you lose sight of the people who make it worth leaving behind. Just… keep that in mind, okay?"

For a moment, Jean-Pierre didn't respond. Then he nodded, his expression softening. "You're right. I'll do better."

Adrien clapped him on the shoulder. "That's all anyone can ask."

The two men stood in companionable silence for a while, the stars twinkling above them and the distant hum of crickets filling the night.

* * *

Jean-Pierre lay in bed, staring at the dark ceiling above him. The weight of Adrien's words, Ana's concern, and his own restless thoughts churned in his mind. He tried to find solace in the rhythmic breathing of Ana beside him, but it only deepened the ache in his chest. He loved her and their children more than anything, but how could he make her see that his search for meaning wasn't a distraction, but an extension of that love?

By the time the first rays of sunlight crept into the room, he had made up his mind. He would not let this fester in silence.

***

Ana was in the kitchen, her robe tied loosely around her waist as she prepared breakfast. The children's laughter echoed faintly from the garden, where Giselle and Pascal were already playing. Jean-Pierre entered; his face drawn but resolute.

"Ana," he began softly, and she turned, startled by the gravity in his tone.

"What is it?" she asked, setting down the knife she'd been using to slice bread.

Jean-Pierre approached her, taking her hands in his. "I didn't sleep last night," he admitted. "I kept thinking about what Adrien said, about what you're feeling, and I realised I can't keep this inside anymore."

Ana's brow creased, concern flashing across her face. "Jean-Pierre…"

He held up a hand, silencing her gently. "Let me finish. Ana, I love you. I love you and the kids more than I can put into words. You're my whole world, my reason for everything. That's why I need you to understand why this is so important to me."

He paused, his voice tightening with emotion. "This research… it's not just a project. It's a way for me to connect with the men who came before me—the men who built the foundation for the life we have now. Louis and Jacques, and so many others—they were brave, Ana. They faced impossible odds, and they stood for something bigger than themselves. I want to understand their courage and their sacrifices. I want to honour them, and in some small way, I want to be worthy of the legacy they left behind."

Ana's eyes softened, but she said nothing, letting him continue.

"This isn't about neglecting you or the kids," he said earnestly. "It's about being the best version of myself for you, for them, and for this place. I'm the heir to the winery, the château, and everything that comes with it. I want to do it proud—to be the kind of man who carries our family's legacy forward with respect and integrity."

His voice cracked slightly as he added, "I want to be brave like Louis and Jacques, but I would never let anything come between us. Nothing will ever matter more to me than you and the children."

Tears welled in Ana's eyes, and she reached up to cup his face. "Oh, Jean-Pierre," she whispered. "I've never doubted your love for us. I know how much this means to you, and I admire your passion. I just… I worry about you; about how much you carry on your shoulders. You don't have to bear it all alone."

He closed his eyes briefly, leaning into her touch. "I know, and I'm sorry if I've made you feel like I'm slipping away. I'll do better, Ana. I'll make sure you and the kids always come first."

She smiled through her tears, pulling him into a tight embrace. "I trust you, Jean-Pierre. And I'm proud of you—for everything you're doing."

For a moment, they simply held each other, the morning light streaming into the kitchen and casting a golden glow around them.

From outside, Giselle's voice rang out, calling for her *Papa*. Jean-Pierre pulled back, his expression softening.

"Let's go have breakfast. As long as I have you and the kids, I'll always know where I belong."

Ana smiled, taking his hand. "And we'll always be here for you, no matter what."

Together, they stepped into the garden, ready to face the day as a family, stronger and more united than ever.

Chapter 21

The air was crisp and cool as Jean-Pierre parked his car at the edge of the dense forest, just a few kilometres from the coordinates he'd deciphered. The journey had been quiet, his mind swirling with possibilities about what lay ahead. Adrien sat beside him, a steadying presence, while Chantelle insisted on coming along, refusing to let her brother take on this mysterious endeavour alone.

The three stepped out into the stillness of the woods. Jean-Pierre held the printed map in one hand and a flashlight in the other. "This is it," he said quietly, nodding towards a faint trail that wound through the trees.

Adrien adjusted his jacket. "Lead the way, but let's stay sharp. If anyone went through the trouble of hiding something out here, they probably didn't want it easily found."

Chantelle gave a small nod, her face etched with both curiosity and unease.

As they followed the trail, the trees thickened, their branches intertwining like ancient sentinels guarding the secrets within. The coordinates led them to a clearing where a dilapidated stone structure stood, its entrance partially obscured by moss and vines.

Jean-Pierre paused, taking in the sight. "It's older than I expected," he murmured. "Almost medieval."

"It might have been repurposed during the war," Chantelle suggested.

Adrien shone his flashlight over the structure. "Looks like a vault. Let's see if it's locked."

The trio approached cautiously. Jean-Pierre found a heavy iron door set into the stone, rusted but still intact. On the door was an emblem, faded with time but faintly recognisable—a French Resistance symbol, paired with an inscription:

Pour ceux qui ont risqué tout (For those who risked everything).

Jean-Pierre's breath caught. "This is it."

With a deep breath, he pushed against the door. It groaned but held firm. Adrien stepped forward, gripping the handle alongside him.

Together, they managed to force it open with a grinding scrape. The air that wafted out was cold and damp, carrying the scent of earth and history.

Inside, the space was small, the walls lined with wooden shelves. On those shelves were stacks of papers, leather-bound notebooks, and metal boxes. Jean-Pierre stepped in first, his flashlight illuminating the treasure trove of documents.

Chantelle followed; her voice hushed with awe. "It's a record… of something significant."

Jean-Pierre picked up one of the notebooks, carefully opening its fragile cover. The name inscribed on the first page made his heart skip a beat: *Louis Dupont.*

"That's Louis' name," he said, his voice barely above a whisper.

Chantelle peered over his shoulder. "Our grandfather?"

Jean-Pierre nodded, his hands trembling slightly as he turned the pages. The entries were meticulous, written in a firm, deliberate hand. Each detailed covert mission carried out during the war—supply routes, safe houses, coded messages, and even lists of names.

Adrien leaned against the doorframe, scanning the contents of a nearby shelf. "He wasn't just involved in the Resistance. He was a key figure. A strategist."

Jean-Pierre's mind raced as he processed the significance of what they'd uncovered. "He wasn't just a farmer or a vintner. He was… leading operations. Look at this," he said, pointing to a detailed map with routes marked in red. "These are smuggling paths. He must've coordinated movements for the Resistance."

Chantelle picked up a separate document, her eyes widening as she read. "There's a list of people he helped escape. These are families that were saved."

The gravity of the discovery settled over them, the weight of history pressing against their chests.

Adrien broke the silence. "Jean-Pierre, this is incredible, but it's also dangerous. These documents could attract the wrong kind of attention if anyone finds out about them."

Jean-Pierre nodded, his resolve hardening. "We'll take what we can carry and secure it at the château. The rest stays hidden until we know what to do with it."

They worked quickly, carefully packing the most delicate and significant documents into a bag. Among the items, they found a sealed envelope addressed to *La Famille Dupont.*
Jean-Pierre held it up, his heart pounding. "This was meant for us."

As he tucked the envelope into the bag, a distant sound broke the stillness of the forest—voices, faint but growing louder. Adrien motioned for silence, his eyes narrowing as he listened.
"Someone's coming," he whispered.

They extinguished their flashlights, retreating deeper into the vault's shadows. Through the narrow crack of the open door, they saw two figures approaching, their voices carrying on the night air.

"Are you sure this is the place?" one of them asked, his tone impatient.

"Positive," the other replied. "The Dupont family's tied to this area. If they're digging into the past, this is where they'll end up."

Jean-Pierre's pulse quickened. He exchanged a glance with Adrien, who nodded subtly.

The strangers lingered outside; their conversation muffled but tense. After what felt like an eternity, they moved on, their footsteps fading into the distance.

Adrien exhaled slowly. "They were looking for this place."

Jean-Pierre's jaw tightened. "And for us."

As the trio emerged from the vault, Chantelle spoke first. "We need to be careful. Whoever they are, they know more than we do right now."

Jean-Pierre nodded. "We'll secure these documents and figure out our next steps. This isn't just about our family anymore—it's bigger than that."

As they made their way back to the car, the weight of the vault's revelations settled over them. The Dupont family's wartime legacy was no longer a distant memory but a living thread, binding them to the courage and sacrifices of those who came before.

For Jean-Pierre, it was clear: the past wasn't just history—it was a call to action, one he could no longer ignore.

Chapter 22

The Dupont family gathered in the château's study, the air thick with tension. A fire crackled in the hearth, but its warmth did little to ease the chill of intrigue laced with unease that had settled over them. Jean-Pierre stood by the window; his silhouette outlined against the twilight. On the desk behind him, the bag of documents retrieved from the vault lay unopened, a tangible reminder of the secrets they had unearthed.

Marcel sat in his favourite armchair, his hands clasped in front of him, his expression inscrutable. Genevieve perched on the sofa, her fingers wrapped tightly around a steaming cup of tea, her knuckles white. Chantelle and Adrien sat together on the loveseat, their presence a quiet but firm support for Jean-Pierre. Ana stood near the door, her gaze shifting between her husband and her father-in-law, a flicker of worry in her eyes.

The silence was broken by Marcel's voice, low and deliberate. "Jean-Pierre, you've brought us to a crossroads. This investigation of yours… it's not just about uncovering history anymore. It's about the safety of this family."

Jean-Pierre turned to face him; his expression resolute. "I understand the risks, *Papa*. But what we've found—it's important. Louis Dupont's work wasn't just resistance; it was salvation for so many people. His story deserves to be told."

Genevieve set her cup down with a soft clink. "And at what cost, Jean-Pierre? Have you considered what might happen if those documents fall into the wrong hands? You three already had strangers snooping around the vault. What if they come here next?"

Chantelle leaned forward, her voice calm but firm. "*Maman*, I get what you're saying. But isn't it also dangerous to leave this in the dark? We can't pretend it doesn't exist."

Adrien nodded in agreement. "This isn't just about family pride or curiosity. These documents might contain information that could rewrite local history. It's bigger than us."

Marcel raised a hand, silencing them all. "Enough. This is not a debate I entered lightly." He turned his piercing gaze on Jean-Pierre. "Do you realise what you're asking of us? You want this family to shoulder the weight of a legacy that nearly destroyed those who carried it during the war."

Jean-Pierre's jaw tightened. "I'm not asking for blind support. I'm asking for trust. Trust that I'll protect this family and honour our history."

Marcel sighed heavily, rubbing his temples. "Jean-Pierre, you have always been steadfast in your convictions, but this... This could expose us to dangers we cannot foresee."

Genevieve placed a hand on Marcel's arm. "We've faced challenges before, Marcel. We've come through them stronger as a family. But this time, it feels different. The world isn't as forgiving as it once was."

Ana spoke softly, drawing their attention. "Maybe it's not about forgiveness. Maybe it's about responsibility. Louis Dupont's story is part of who we are, all of us. And if the truth can help others understand what people like him sacrificed, isn't that worth considering?"

Marcel looked at her, his expression softening. "Ana, you speak with conviction, but you don't yet understand the cost of such a responsibility. It changes you."

Adrien cleared his throat, his tone measured. "With respect, Marcel, maybe that's why Jean-Pierre is the right person for this. He's grounded in who he is because of the foundation you and Genevieve built. If anyone can honour Louis' legacy and protect the family, it's him."

The room fell silent again, the weight of Adrien's words hanging in the air. Marcel leaned back in his chair; his gaze fixed on the fire. Finally, he spoke, his voice quiet but steady. "Jean-Pierre, if you're determined to pursue this, you will do so with caution and the understanding that this family's safety is paramount. You'll have my support—not because I think this is wise, but because I trust you to do what is right."

Jean-Pierre's shoulders relaxed slightly, though his expression remained serious. "Thank you, *Papa*. I won't let you down."

Genevieve looked at her son, her eyes filled with a mix of pride and worry. "Jean-Pierre, promise me you'll keep Ana and the children out of this. They shouldn't have to bear the burden of what might come."

Jean-Pierre nodded. "I promise."

Chantelle stood, crossing the room to place a hand on her brother's arm. "We're in this together, Jean. Whatever happens, we'll face it as a family."

Adrien followed, standing beside her. "We've got your back."

Marcel watched them, his stern expression softening into something more resigned. "Then let it be so. But remember this: the past has a way of haunting the present. Be prepared for what you might find."

The meeting dissolved into quieter conversations, the family processing the decision in their respective ways. Jean-Pierre stayed by the window, looking out into the night. The stars above the vineyard seemed brighter than usual, a reminder of the legacy he now carried.

For better or worse, the path was set. And as Jean-Pierre turned back to his family, he knew he would need their strength as much as his own to face whatever lay ahead.

Chapter 23

Jean-Pierre arrived at the vineyard early, the crisp morning air heavy with the earthy scent of soil and dew. As he approached the rows of vines, his heart sank. Sections of the vineyard had been trampled, their delicate tendrils snapped, and tools lay scattered as if someone had ransacked the area.

Adrien, who had arrived shortly after to lend a hand, whistled low as he took in the damage. "This wasn't an accident," he said grimly, crouching to examine the wreckage. "Someone did this deliberately."

Jean-Pierre nodded, a tightness in his chest growing. "I thought the vineyard might be spared from all this," he said quietly. "Clearly, I was wrong."

As they worked to salvage what they could, Marcel appeared, his face lined with worry. He had heard the commotion and come to see the damage for himself. Jean-Pierre explained what they'd found, and Marcel's expression darkened. "This isn't just vandalism," Marcel said. "It's a message."

Jean-Pierre looked up sharply, but before he could respond, Ana approached them, a piece of paper in her hand. "This was tucked under the windshield wiper of your truck," she said, her voice trembling slightly.

Jean-Pierre unfolded the note, his pulse quickening. The words, scrawled in blocky, uneven handwriting, read:

STOP DIGGING INTO THE PAST. WE'RE WATCHING YOUR FAMILY.

Adrien leaned over his shoulder to read. "Well, that's subtle," he said dryly, though his jaw tightened. "Whoever this is, they're not bluffing."

Marcel took the note, studying it carefully. "This isn't just about the vineyard or even the past. They're making it personal—threatening the people you care about."

Ana wrapped her arms around herself, her face pale. "This is serious, Jean-Pierre. What if it's not just a warning? What if they escalate?"

Jean-Pierre felt a wave of guilt. He'd been so focused on uncovering the truth about Louis Dupont and the family's history that he hadn't considered the full extent of the risks involved. Now, it seemed his investigation was drawing danger closer to the very people he wanted to protect.

"We'll report this to the authorities," Marcel said firmly, placing a hand on Jean-Pierre's shoulder. "And we'll take precautions here at the château. But you need to think carefully about how much further you want to push this."

Adrien, standing nearby, crossed his arms. "You're not alone in this, Jean-Pierre. Whatever decision you make, we'll face it together. But don't underestimate what these people are capable of."

Jean-Pierre nodded, though his mind was racing. The note wasn't going to deter him—not entirely—but it was a stark reminder of the stakes involved. He had to find a way to protect his family while pursuing the answers that had eluded them for so long.

Later that evening, as he stood at the edge of the vineyard, staring out over the damaged rows, he felt the weight of the decision pressing down on him. The vineyard, the château, his family—all of it was part of a legacy he couldn't ignore. But at what cost?

"Whoever you are," he muttered under his breath, gripping the note tightly, "you won't scare me away. Not yet."

Chapter 24

Jean-Pierre sat in his study, surrounded by a growing mound of papers, old photographs, and books. The fire crackled in the hearth, casting flickering shadows across the walls lined with vintage maps and family heirlooms. Among the artefacts were the recently discovered coded letters dug out of a secret vault, their faded ink whispering secrets of a bygone era. These letters, tied to Louis Dupont and Jacques Lambert, seemed to hold answers that could reshape everything Jean-Pierre thought he knew about his family's history.

With a deep breath, Jean-Pierre turned to the first letter. It had taken days of meticulous effort to decipher the intricate code. The cypher, a mix of substitution and transposition techniques, reflected the ingenuity required during wartime to protect vital information. Using a combination of intuition, historical research, and trial and error, Jean-Pierre finally unravelled the cryptic symbols.

The first decoded message read:

"Coordinates secured. Lambert will deliver. Resistance efforts align with Allied command."

Jean-Pierre's heart raced. This confirmed not only Louis Dupont's collaboration with Jacques Lambert but also hinted at Lambert's critical role in connecting the local Resistance with broader Allied strategies. The next few letters revealed similar themes — strategic plans, supply routes, and encrypted lists of collaborators. Each word painted a vivid picture of clandestine operations carried out under the ever-present threat of discovery.

But as Jean-Pierre delved deeper, a more complex narrative began to emerge. A particular letter caught his attention. Its tone was different, almost conflicted:

"Lambert's dual role compromises our efforts. Trust is a luxury we cannot afford."

Jean-Pierre leaned back in his chair, the weight of the revelation pressing down on him. Jacques Lambert, a trusted ally of Louis Dupont, was not merely a Resistance operative. He had been navigating a perilous path, acting as a double agent. The implications were staggering. Had Lambert's dual roles endangered the Resistance? Or had his actions served a greater purpose, perhaps manipulating the enemy to the Resistance's advantage?

Driven by curiosity and unease, Jean-Pierre continued decoding late into the night. His desk became a battlefield of half-emptied coffee cups and hastily scribbled notes. Each deciphered letter added a new layer to the story, painting Jacques Lambert as a man caught between loyalties, walking a tightrope where a single misstep could have been fatal.

One letter revealed Lambert's connection to the Gestapo:

"Meeting arranged under pretence. Information shared is deliberate misinformation. Objectives remain intact."

Jean-Pierre's breath caught. Lambert's duplicity was not born of betrayal but of strategy. By feeding false information to the Gestapo, he had misled the enemy, buying crucial time for Resistance operations. Yet, the risk was unimaginable. If exposed, Lambert would have faced torture and execution, and his connection to Louis Dupont could have brought the entire Dupont family into peril.

As the hours passed, Jean-Pierre pieced together a fragmented yet compelling narrative. Louis Dupont had worked closely with Jacques Lambert, orchestrating missions that ranged from sabotage to intelligence gathering. Together, they had orchestrated daring acts of defiance, including the derailment of a German supply train and the rescue of imprisoned Resistance fighters. But the letters also hinted at moments of tension, where Lambert's methods and secrets had sown seeds of doubt among his allies.

One particularly poignant letter, written by Louis Dupont, addressed these doubts:

"Jacques walks a path few can understand. His actions, though shrouded in shadows, have saved countless lives. We trust him, not because we understand him, but because we see the results of his courage."

Jean-Pierre paused, the letter trembling in his hands. The words offered a rare glimpse into his grandfather's psyche. Louis had been a man of unyielding faith in his comrades, even when faced with uncertainty. The sentiment resonated deeply with Jean-Pierre, who found himself grappling with similar questions of trust and legacy in his investigation.

As dawn broke, casting a pale light over the study, Jean-Pierre stood and stretched. He glanced at the family vineyard through the window, its rows of vines standing resolute against the Alpine backdrop. The land, so intertwined with his family's identity, now seemed like a silent witness to the extraordinary events of the past.

Later that morning, Jean-Pierre called a family meeting to share his findings. The Dupont family gathered in the château's sitting room; the atmosphere charged with anticipation. Marcel, Genevieve, Chantelle, Adrien, Ana, and even the children, Giselle and Pascal, listened intently as Jean-Pierre recounted the letters' revelations.

"Louis Dupont and Jacques Lambert were more than just Resistance fighters," Jean-Pierre began, his voice steady but filled with emotion. "They were architects of a movement, risking everything to defy tyranny. But Lambert's role as a double agent adds a complexity I didn't expect. It's both inspiring and unsettling."

Genevieve's expression turned sombre. "The weight of such secrets must have been unbearable," she said softly. "Imagine living with that kind of constant fear and uncertainty, knowing that one wrong move could doom everyone you care about."

Marcel nodded. "It explains the silence that followed the war. They carried these stories to their graves, perhaps believing that sparing us the details was an act of protection."

Chantelle leaned forward; her medical instincts evident in her analytical tone. "But what about the psychological toll? Lambert's duplicity, even if strategic, must have been isolating. And Louis… how did he reconcile his trust in Lambert with the knowledge of his double life?"

Jean-Pierre sighed. "I don't have all the answers yet. But these letters suggest that, despite the risks, their partnership was instrumental in some of the Resistance's greatest successes."

Adrien, ever the pragmatist, interjected. "And what does this mean for us now? These discoveries are incredible, but they also place a target on your back. You're uncovering truths that some might prefer to remain buried."

The room fell silent, the weight of Adrien's words sinking in. Ana reached for Jean-Pierre's hand, her touch a grounding force. "Whatever comes of this, we will face them. The Dupont family has weathered storms before, and we will again."

As the family dispersed, Jean-Pierre returned to his study, determined to continue his work. He knew the path ahead was fraught with challenges, but the revelations about Louis Dupont and Jacques Lambert had ignited a fire within him. Their story was not just a chapter in history; it was a testament to resilience, courage, and the enduring power of truth.

Sitting at his desk, Jean-Pierre picked up the next letter, ready to uncover the next piece of the puzzle. As he worked, the faint echoes of the past seemed to whisper around him, urging him forward. The journey was far from over, but Jean-Pierre knew one thing for certain: he would honour the legacy of Louis Dupont and Jacques Lambert, no matter the cost.

Mario Zatta

Chapter 25

The midday sun filtered through the sprawling vineyards, dappling the château's grand dining room with patterns of light and shadow. Jean-Pierre sat at the large oak table, surrounded by a growing mountain of documents, letters, and maps. His hair was dishevelled and his forehead creased in concentration as he pored over yet another encoded letter. The faint hum of conversation in the adjacent kitchen broke the quiet, but he hardly noticed.

Adrien leaned against the doorframe, arms crossed, his usual relaxed demeanour replaced with a look of concern. Ana stood beside him, her expression mirroring his worry. After exchanging a glance, Adrien cleared his throat. Jean-Pierre didn't look up.

"Jean-Pierre," Adrien said gently but firmly. "We need to talk." Jean-Pierre paused, pen poised in midair, before reluctantly turning his gaze to them. "What is it?"

Adrien stepped into the room, motioning for Ana to follow. "Look, we're all for uncovering history, especially something as important as this. But… you're losing yourself in it. It's starting to take over everything and the sabotage in the vineyard could be a precursor for worse to come."

Ana nodded; her voice soft but steady. "Adrien's right. The vineyard, the family… even Giselle and Pascal. They miss you. I miss you." Her eyes shimmered with unshed tears. "You're here with us, but it feels like your mind is somewhere else. I know we've gone through this but it's like it's fallen on deaf ears."

Jean-Pierre's face softened, guilt flickering in his hazel eyes. He set down the pen and leaned back in his chair, rubbing his temples. "I didn't realise it was that bad."

"It's not just about the time you're spending," Adrien said, taking a seat across from him. "It's the risk. You found that note, the sabotage at the vineyard and they came looking for us at the vault—whoever's behind this isn't messing around. This isn't just history anymore, Jean-Pierre. It's dangerous."

"You're both exaggerating," Jean-Pierre said, though his tone lacked conviction. "This is about understanding who we are, and where we come from. It's important."

Ana reached across the table, placing a hand on his. "And we're not saying it's not. But at what cost? You're not just a historian. You're a husband, a father, a brother. You have responsibilities here, now."

The weight of her words hung in the air. Jean-Pierre's gaze drifted to the stack of papers, then out the window where his children played near the edge of the vineyard. His chest tightened at the sight.

Before he could respond, Chantelle entered the room, her presence immediately easing the tension. "What's going on?" she asked, glancing between the three of them.

Adrien gestured towards Jean-Pierre. "We're trying to make him see reason."

"And I'm being ganged up on," Jean-Pierre muttered, though his lips twitched in a faint smile.

Chantelle pulled out a chair and sat down beside him. "Jean, they're not wrong. You've been… distracted. And with good reason, given everything you've uncovered. But maybe it's time to step back and think about how you're balancing this. You're not in this alone. If you're determined to see this through then let's share the burden"

Jean-Pierre sighed, running a hand through his hair. "I just feel like I'm so close to something. Every time I think about stopping, it's like I'd be betraying their memory. Louis, Jacques… everything they risked, everything they sacrificed."

Chantelle's expression softened. "Nobody's asking you to stop and you're not betraying them by taking care of the present. If anything, they'd want you to protect what they fought for. Family. Safety. A future."

Adrien leaned forward. "Exactly. No one's saying you should stop. Just… slow down. Be careful. Let us help you."

Jean-Pierre's gaze met Adrien's, then Ana's, and finally Chantelle's.

He saw the love and concern in their eyes, and it struck a chord deep within him. He nodded slowly. "You're right. I've been so focused on the past that I've been neglecting the present."

Ana's shoulders relaxed, and she offered him a small smile. "We just want you to be here with us, Jean."

"I'll try," he said, his voice barely above a whisper. "I can't promise to stop entirely, but I'll try to find a better balance."

Chantelle reached over, squeezing his hand. "That's all we're asking for."

For a moment, silence settled over the room, filled with unspoken understanding. Then Adrien broke it with a teasing grin. "Besides, if you don't start showing up more in the vineyard, I might have to take your job."

Jean-Pierre chuckled, the tension in his shoulders easing slightly. "You're welcome to try. But let me warn you, those vines have a mind of their own."

Ana laughed, her smile reaching her eyes for the first time that day. "Now that I'd like to see."

The four of them sat together, the weight of the conversation lifting. Outside, the laughter of Giselle and Pascal echoed through the vineyard, a reminder of what truly mattered.

Mario Zatta

Chapter 26

The morning sun filtered through the vineyard's rows, casting long shadows across the dew-soaked ground. Jean-Pierre slid into his car, an old but reliable Range Rover, to head into town for supplies. As he turned the ignition, a sharp, metallic screech erupted from beneath the vehicle, followed by a heavy clunk. Alarmed, he immediately turned off the engine and stepped out to investigate.

Kneeling, he peered under the car. A thick cable dangled loose, severed cleanly, and bolts that should have secured the undercarriage were missing. A cold wave of realisation swept over him—this wasn't 'wear and tear'. Someone had tampered with his car.

Jean-Pierre stood up, his mind racing. He scanned the vineyard, its serene beauty now tinged with an undercurrent of menace. The thought of danger encroaching on his family's sanctuary made his stomach churn.

He called Adrien, who was still at the château.

"Adrien, I need you down here at the west lot. Something's wrong with my car."

"On my way," Adrien replied without hesitation.

Minutes later, Adrien jogged into view, his face etched with concern. "What happened?"

Jean-Pierre pointed to the car. "The brake lines have been cut, and some bolts are missing. Someone's been messing with it."

Adrien crouched to inspect the damage. "This wasn't an accident. Someone wanted to make sure you couldn't stop—or worse."

Jean-Pierre clenched his fists. "This has gone too far. First the note, now this. Whoever these people are, they're escalating."

That evening, the château was unusually tense. Marcel and Genevieve gathered the family in the sitting room, a rare event during the harvest season. Jean-Pierre recounted the sabotage, his voice laced with frustration and fear.

"This isn't just about me anymore. They're targeting us—our home, our livelihood."

Marcel's brow channelled deeply; his usually calm demeanour shaken. "And the strangers in the vineyard?"

Adrien chimed in. "I've seen them too. Twice now, men lurking near the south gate. They left as soon as I approached, but it didn't feel right."

Genevieve placed a reassuring hand on Jean-Pierre's shoulder. "We must protect ourselves. Marcel, do you think it's time to involve the authorities?"

Marcel hesitated. The Dupont family had always valued their privacy, but this was different. "I'll contact a trusted friend in the Swiss police. We need protection, but we also need discretion."

* * *

The next morning, an unmarked police car pulled into the château's driveway. Officer Matthias Keller, an old friend of Marcel's, stepped out.

"Marcel," Matthias greeted with a firm handshake. "I came as soon as I could. Tell me everything."

Marcel led Matthias to his study, where Jean-Pierre joined them. They laid out the incidents—the threatening note, the tampered car, and the strangers in the vineyard.

Matthias listened intently, his sharp eyes narrowing as he took notes. "This isn't random," he concluded. "Someone is deliberately trying to intimidate your family. Do you have any idea who might be behind this?"

Jean-Pierre exchanged a glance with Marcel. "It could be connected to my investigation into Louis Dupont's wartime activities. We've uncovered some sensitive information about his role in the Resistance—and possibly some enemies he made along the way."

Matthias nodded gravely. "Digging into the past can stir up things best left buried. But that doesn't justify this. I'll assign plainclothes officers to patrol the area and increase surveillance around the château and vineyard."

That afternoon, as the family gathered for lunch, the mood was sombre. Giselle and Pascal, sensing the tension, remained unusually quiet. Chantelle broke the silence.

"We need to stick together through this," she said, her tone firm. "Whatever is happening, we can't let it tear us apart."

Adrien nodded. "Agreed. But we also need to be vigilant. Whoever is behind this clearly doesn't want us to uncover the truth."

Jean-Pierre, his jaw tight, stared out the window towards the vineyard. "I'm not stopping. Louis deserves to have his story told, and our family deserves to know the truth. But I won't put any of you at risk. I'll be more cautious."

Ana reached across the table, her hand finding Jean-Pierre's. "We'll face this together. You're not alone in this, Jean-Pierre."

Marcel then spoke, a rare flicker of determination in his eyes. "To the Dupont family—stronger together. Whatever comes, we will endure."

The family all nodded subtly, the unspoken resolve uniting them.

Outside, the vineyard stretched towards the horizon, its beauty marred by the shadows of the unknown. But inside the château, the family stood firm, ready to face whatever lay ahead.

Mario Zatta

Chapter 27

The atmosphere in the château had been heavy for days. The unspoken weight of threats and uncertainty pressed on each family member, especially Jean-Pierre. Chantelle, ever perceptive, decided it was time for a change.

"Right, we need a break," she declared loudly, her voice carrying into the sitting room where the family had gathered. "We've all been cooped up, worried, and tense. We need some fresh air. Let's go outside and enjoy nature. I'll pack a picnic."

The suggestion immediately lit up the room. Giselle's face brightened, and Pascal, sitting by his grandfather's feet, jumped up. "Can we help, *Tata*?"

Chantelle smiled. "Of course! Go grab the basket from the pantry." She moved towards the kitchen, already pulling fresh bread and jars of preserves from the shelves.

Genevieve, her spirits lifted, joined her, rolling up her sleeves. "What a wonderful idea. Let's make it a real feast," she said, slicing wedges of Gruyère and Emmental cheeses.

It seemed to take a while to sink in but slowly each one stood up in turn. Ana appeared beside Genevieve, gathering napkins and plates. "I'll prepare the cold meats," she said, reaching for the selection of cured ham, *Bündnerfleisch*, and smoked sausages. Chantelle worked quickly, delegating tasks to everyone as the energy in the château shifted. Even Marcel was drawn in, filling a thermos with coffee while Adrien gathered a bottle of white wine and glasses.

The group set off an hour later, laughter and chatter replacing the solemn quiet that had gripped them earlier.

On arrival, they followed a well-worn path towards the forest at the mountain's base. Within a quarter of an hour, they reached the forest, and as they ventured deeper into it, the ground became a tapestry of vibrant greens and browns, the forest floor dotted with a thick layer of leaf litter and soft moss that cushioned their footsteps. Towering trees, their trunks gnarled and ancient, stretched skyward, their branches intertwined overhead to form a natural canopy that filtered the sunlight into dappled patterns on the ground. The air was rich with the scent of pine and damp earth, while the melodic sounds of chirping birds and rustling leaves accompanied their journey. They navigated over smooth, moss-covered stones that jutted up from the earth, carefully picking their footing as they crossed bubbling streams that wound through the underbrush. Here and there, delicate wildflowers peeked out from between the roots, adding splashes of colour to the lush greenery, while the occasional flicker of movement hinted at the presence of small creatures observing their passage. Each step brought them closer to the heart of the forest, where the whisper of the wind and the distant sound of a waterfall beckoned them forward.

They continued and followed the path, the children now skipping ahead with Adrien, who entertained them with an animated retelling of *Little Red Riding Hood*.

"The big bad wolf could be anywhere in these woods," Adrien teased, his tone light but playful. Pascal clutched his sister's hand, his wide eyes scanning the trees. "But don't worry," Adrien added, winking. "I'll protect you."

The forest embraced them in its tranquillity, the earthy scent of moss and pine needles mingling with the crisp mountain air. Sunlight filtered through the canopy, creating a mosaic of light and shadow on the forest floor. Birds chirped overhead, and the distant sound of a bubbling brook added to the serenity.

Genevieve's sharp eyes lit up when she spotted a cluster of mushrooms near the path. "Look! Chanterelles!" she exclaimed, crouching to pick a few. "These will be perfect for dinner tonight." Jean-Pierre, walking silently behind the group, paused to take in the moment. The forest's beauty was undeniable, yet the ever-present tension of the threats weighed heavily on his mind. Still, seeing his family laugh and bond softened the edges of his worry, if only for a moment.

The group eventually emerged into a clearing, a breathtaking spot with panoramic views of the Swiss countryside. Rolling green hills stretched into the distance, dotted with chalets and grazing cattle. Snow-capped peaks framed the horizon, their majestic presence grounding the scene in timeless splendour.

"This is perfect," Genevieve said, spreading a blanket on the soft grass. The children helped arrange the food, placing loaves of crusty rye bread, cheeses, and an assortment of cold meats in the centre. Chantelle unpacked jars of homemade preserves, while Ana poured fresh apple cider into small cups for the children.

The smells of the picnic mingled with the forest air—the nutty aroma of Gruyère, the smoky scent of *Bündnerfleisch*, and the sweet tang of apricot jam. There were also flaky pastries filled with spinach and cheese, hard-boiled eggs sprinkled with salt, and slices of fruitcake from Genevieve's kitchen.

Everyone settled on the blanket, the tension of the past days melting away as they enjoyed the meal. Adrien regaled the group with light-hearted tales, his voice carrying easily over the rustle of leaves. Pascal and Giselle giggled between bites, their faces sticky with jam.

Jean-Pierre sat beside his father; his mind still troubled but his heart warmed by the scene around him. His gaze drifted over the clearing, the vibrant greens of the grass, the distant azure sky, and the golden light that bathed the landscape.

Marcel, sensing the moment, raised his glass of white wine. His voice, though steady, carried an unmistakable warmth. "We'll get through this," he said, looking around at his family.

Everyone paused, their glasses raised in silent agreement. Smiles spread across their faces as they clinked glasses, a quiet but powerful gesture of unity. Ana shifted her gaze from Marcel, placing her hand on Jean-Pierre's thigh, and raising the glass to her lips, gave him a reassuring smile.

For a while, they all sat in silence, savouring the view and each other's presence. The Swiss countryside stretched before them; its beauty undiminished by the challenges they faced.

In that moment, the Dupont family found solace in their togetherness, drawing strength from the bonds that held them close.

Chapter 28

Jean-Pierre sat at his desk in the study, the flickering light from the antique desk lamp casting long shadows over the parchment-like pages before him. The smell of old paper and leather-bound books filled the room, mingling with the faint aroma of oak from the château's aged walls. Spread across the desk were meticulously decoded letters, their cryptic messages now unravelled into haunting truths. Each line of text seemed to pulse with the weight of history, pulling Jean-Pierre deeper into the moral quandaries of Jacques Lambert—Louis Dupont's wartime ally.

The letters painted a picture of Jacques as a man divided. He had been a hero to some, a traitor to others, and a mystery even to those who trusted him most. Jean-Pierre leaned back in his chair, staring at the ceiling as he tried to reconcile the man depicted in these pages with the figure he had imagined.

One letter stood out. It was addressed to Louis Dupont and detailed a decision Jacques had faced during the height of the war. The Resistance had intercepted information about a planned German raid on a nearby village suspected of harbouring fugitives. Jacques had two options: warn the villagers, risking the exposure of their entire network, or remain silent, ensuring the Resistance could continue their broader efforts.

The words were written with a trembling hand, the ink blotched in places where the pen had lingered too long.

"Louis," the letter read, *"we make choices not because they are right, but because they are necessary. I chose silence, and the village burned."*

Jean-Pierre's heart sank as he imagined the horror Jacques must have felt. How could a man live with such a choice?

The next morning, unable to shake the letter's impact, Jean-Pierre sought solace in the vineyard. The familiar rows of vines stretching across the horizon were usually a source of comfort, but today they seemed to echo the tangled lines of Jacques' moral conflicts. He walked slowly, letting the crisp mountain air clear his mind. His boots crunched against the gravel path, and the faint rustle of leaves whispered around him as if the vines themselves were murmuring their secrets.

Chantelle found him there, her face etched with concern. "You've been quiet," she said softly, falling into step beside him. "Is it about the letters?"

Jean-Pierre nodded, passing her the most damning of Jacques' writings. She scanned the lines, her expression tightening as she read. When she finally looked up, her green eyes met his, filled with a mixture of empathy and unease.
"These aren't just tactical decisions," she said, her voice barely above a whisper. "They're sacrifices. Every choice he made carried a cost."

"Sacrifices?" Jean-Pierre echoed bitterly. "Tell that to the families of that village."

Chantelle sighed. "And if he had warned them, how many more lives might have been lost? The Resistance could have been destroyed. These are the kinds of choices people in war have to make. It's not fair, and it's not clean."

He shook his head, frustration bubbling to the surface. "It feels like everything I uncover only complicates things. I wanted to understand our family's legacy, but all I've found is a web of contradictions."

"Maybe that's the legacy," she said gently. "That they were human, and they did the best they could under impossible circumstances."

***

Jean-Pierre returned to the study later that evening, determined to make sense of Jacques' actions. He pored over more letters, piecing together fragments of missions and plans. Jacques had been a master of misdirection, working as a double agent to gather intelligence from the Germans while feeding them false information. It was a perilous dance, one that required him to betray confidences on both sides.

One letter revealed how Jacques had orchestrated the destruction of a German supply convoy by leaking its route to the Allies. The success of the mission had saved countless lives, but it had also led to the execution of a Resistance informant within the German ranks. Jacques had expressed his anguish in painfully raw words:

"Her name was Danielle. She trusted me. I gave her up because the mission demanded it. God help me, Louis, but I see her face every night."

Jean-Pierre could almost hear the man's voice in the jagged script. This wasn't the unflinching hero of Resistance lore, nor was it the villain some had accused Jacques of being. He was something in between—a man haunted by his choices, trying to navigate the moral labyrinth of war.

As the night wore on, Jean-Pierre felt a strange kinship with Jacques. He, too, was wrestling with the weight of decisions that could shape not only his family's understanding of their past but also their future. The shadows of the past seemed to stretch into the present, casting doubt and unease over every step of his investigation.

Genevieve appeared in the doorway, her presence a quiet balm to his fraying nerves. "You're still at it," she observed, carrying a steaming cup of tea. She placed it on the desk and sat across from him, her eyes scanning the scattered papers.

"I feel like I'm unravelling a tapestry," Jean-Pierre admitted. "But every thread I pull just reveals another knot."

Genevieve reached for one of the letters, her face softening as she read. "Jacques Lambert was a complicated man," she said. "But aren't we all? War doesn't allow for purity of action. It's messy, and people make choices they're forced into, not because they want to."

Jean-Pierre studied her, realising how much her insight had always grounded their family. "Do you think I'm making a mistake? Digging all this up?"

She shook her head. "Mistake? No. But it's a burden, Jean-Pierre. For you and for everyone around you. Just promise me you'll remember that the past isn't the only thing that matters. The present—the family you've built—is just as important."

Her words lingered long after she left the room. Jean-Pierre gazed at the pile of letters, feeling both the weight of history and the pull of his family's love. He knew he couldn't stop now, but he also realised that the answers he sought wouldn't be found solely in these pages. They lived in the connections between past and present, in the choices he made moving forward, and in the legacy he would leave for those who came after him.

Chapter 29

Jean-Pierre was walking through the vineyard at dusk, the dimming light fading into deep hues of purple and blue. The rows of vines stretched endlessly, their leaves rustling softly in the mountain breeze. He often found solace here, where the land seemed timeless, but tonight, the tranquillity felt fragile. His mind was weighed down by the revelations of the past weeks and the cryptic warning notes that hinted at a lurking danger.

As he reached the far edge of the vineyard, a shadow moved among the trees at the boundary of the property. Jean-Pierre froze. He squinted into the gloom, his heartbeat quickening.

"Who's there?" he called out, his voice steady despite the sudden tension in his chest.

Two figures stepped into view; their faces partially obscured by the dim light. They were dressed plainly, but their presence radiated an air of quiet menace.

"Monsieur Dupont," one of them said, his voice low and deliberate. "We need to talk."

Jean-Pierre instinctively stepped back but held his ground. "Who are you? What do you want?"

The second man, taller and broader, took a step forward. "We represent a group with a vested interest in your family's discretion. You've been asking questions, uncovering things better left buried."

Jean-Pierre's stomach churned, but he kept his expression calm. "If you're referring to my research into my great-grandfather's activities, I have every right to know my family's history."

"It's not just your history," the first man said sharply. "The Duponts weren't acting alone. What they knew, what they did—it intersects with a network that still exists. A network that values its secrecy."

Jean-Pierre's mind raced. This was no mere historical curiosity. He had stumbled into something far more dangerous than he had anticipated.

"And if I don't stop?" he challenged his voice firm despite the growing unease in his chest.

The taller man's gaze hardened. "If you don't stop, you'll bring trouble not just to yourself, but to your family. We've been watching,

Monsieur Dupont. We know about your wife, your children, your parents."

Jean-Pierre's fists clenched at his sides. "Are you threatening my family?"

The first man raised a hand, a mockery of reassurance. "Not a threat. A warning. Stop your investigation, and your family will remain safe. Continue, and we cannot guarantee the same."

Jean-Pierre's heart pounded as he tried to think of a response. Before he could speak, the men turned and disappeared into the shadows as swiftly as they had come, leaving him alone in the deepening twilight.

For a long moment, Jean-Pierre stood frozen, the rustling of the leaves and the distant chirping of crickets the only sounds in the gathering night. He felt as though the ground beneath him had shifted, leaving him unsteady. Questions roared through his mind, each one louder than the last.

What have I done? Who are these people? How deep does this go?

He pressed a hand to his forehead, trying to calm the storm of thoughts.

I can't let them hurt my family. I won't let them. But what am I going to do?

He looked back towards the château, the warm glow of the lights in the distance a stark contrast to the cold dread settling in his chest. His family was there, laughing, eating, living their lives—unaware of the storm that was now swirling around them. He had to protect them, but how? Stopping the investigation felt like surrendering to fear, but continuing meant risking the safety of everyone he loved.

Jean-Pierre clenched his fists, his jaw tightening as resolve began to creep back in.

I need to figure this out. I need to stay ahead of them. If they think they can intimidate me into giving up, they're wrong.

With a deep breath, he turned and began walking back towards the château, each step heavy with the weight of his decision.

***

When Jean-Pierre returned to the château, his face was pale, and his hands were trembling. He found Marcel in the study, poring over correspondence with the Swiss authorities about the recent vandalism at the vineyard.

"What happened?" Marcel asked, alarmed by his son's shaken demeanour.

Jean-Pierre recounted the encounter, his voice tight with anger and fear. When he finished, Marcel's jaw was set, his eyes blazing with a protective fury Jean-Pierre had rarely seen.

"They dare to come onto our land and threaten us?" Marcel growled, slamming his fist onto the desk. "This is unacceptable."

"They called themselves a network," Jean-Pierre said, pacing the room. "They implied that my grandfather's work wasn't just about the Resistance—that it touched something larger, something that still exists."

Marcel leaned back in his chair, rubbing his temples as he processed the revelation. "This changes everything. If this network is still active, they won't stop at warnings."

"We need to protect the family," Jean-Pierre said urgently. "Genevieve, Chantelle, the children—they could be in danger because of me."

"We'll increase security," Marcel said firmly. "I'll contact the authorities again, and explain the seriousness of the situation. But Jean-Pierre…" He paused, his expression grave. "Are you sure you want to continue this? If these men are part of something as dangerous as they claim, is it worth the risk?"

Jean-Pierre met his father's gaze, his resolve hardening. "They're trying to silence me. That tells me there's something important here, something they don't want uncovered. I can't stop now, not when I'm so close to understanding the truth."

Marcel sighed, a mixture of pride and frustration in his eyes. "Then we'll face it together. But promise me you'll be careful. This family has survived too much to be torn apart now."

***

Later that evening, as the family gathered for dinner, Jean-Pierre couldn't shake the memory of the men's warning. His gaze lingered on Pascal and Giselle, their laughter filling the room as they played with Adrien. Genevieve noticed his distraction and placed a reassuring hand on his arm.

"Whatever it is, I'm here for you," she said softly.

Jean-Pierre nodded; his determination renewed.

He would protect his family at all costs, even if it meant delving deeper into the shadows of their legacy.

Mario Zatta

Chapter 30

Genevieve sat on the veranda, her hands cradling a warm mug of herbal tea. The sun had begun its descent, painting the sky with hues of amber and rose. The familiar scent of lavender from the garden mingled with the crisp alpine air. She could hear the faint laughter of her grandchildren playing in the distance, a comforting melody that contrasted starkly with the weight she felt on her heart.

"Marcel," she called softly as her husband stepped outside, carrying a book he had been reading. He looked at her, his eyes filled with concern and understanding. "I've been thinking about the past… about my parents."

Marcel took a seat beside her, his hand gently covering hers. "What's on your mind?"

Genevieve took a deep breath, her gaze fixed on the horizon. "During the war, my parents rarely spoke of what they endured. But there were moments… brief glimpses into their experiences that they couldn't entirely hide. I remember my mother's hands trembling when certain songs played on the radio, and my father's silence whenever the topic of the occupation arose."

Marcel nodded, listening intently as Genevieve's voice wavered with emotion. "One night, when I was a teenager, my mother told me about a family they had hidden in their cellar for months. She said it was the most terrifying yet rewarding time of her life. The fear of being discovered was constant. Every knock at the door, every unfamiliar sound outside, sent shivers down their spines. But they did it because it was the right thing to do."

Genevieve paused, her eyes glistening with unshed tears. "She spoke about the children… two little girls who used to draw pictures on the cellar walls with bits of charcoal my mother gave them. When the family finally left to escape to the next safe house, my mother found one last drawing they had made. It was of our family, holding hands with theirs, standing under a drawing of the sun. She kept that drawing hidden in a tin box until the day she died."

Marcel's grip on her hand tightened. "That's a remarkable legacy of courage and compassion, Genevieve. But I can see why it weighs heavily on you now."

Genevieve turned to face him, her expression a mixture of sorrow and resolve. "Marcel, these stories remind me of the risks people took to protect others. And now, with everything Jean-Pierre is uncovering, I can't help but feel a deep connection between their sacrifices and our current struggles. But at the same time, I'm terrified."

"Terrified of what?" Marcel asked gently.

"Of history repeating itself," Genevieve admitted. "Of our family being dragged into danger because of the past. Jean-Pierre is so driven, so passionate about uncovering the truth, but I worry he doesn't see the full picture. I've always believed in supporting him, in standing by our children no matter what. But how do we balance that with keeping them safe?"

Marcel looked thoughtful, his gaze drifting towards the vineyard where Jean-Pierre often worked tirelessly. "You've always been the one to ground us, Genevieve. Even during the toughest times, your clarity and wisdom have kept this family together. Perhaps now is the time to remind Jean-Pierre of that balance—of honouring the past without letting it consume the present."

Genevieve's lips curved into a faint smile. "He's so much like you, you know. Stubborn, determined, and with a heart bigger than he'll ever admit. I'll talk to him, but not to dissuade him. I just want him to understand the importance of caution and perspective."

Marcel nodded. "And he'll listen because deep down, he knows you're right."

Genevieve's thoughts returned to her parents' stories. She recalled her father's quiet strength, the way he'd sit by the fire, his hands clasped as though in prayer. He never spoke of the lives he'd helped save, but there was a gravity to him that hinted at the weight of those memories. "My father once told me that doing the right thing often comes at a cost. But he also said that the cost of doing nothing is far greater."

"Wise words," Marcel said. "Perhaps that's something Jean-Pierre needs to hear. He's grappling with more than just the past. He's trying to reconcile it with who he is and what he stands for."

Genevieve leaned back, her gaze lifting to the sky where the first stars had begun to twinkle. "I'll tell him. But I'll also remind him that he's not alone in this. That we're a family, and we face these challenges together. Just as my parents faced theirs."

Marcel wrapped an arm around her shoulders, pulling her close. "And we'll get through this, Genevieve. Just as they did."

The sound of footsteps interrupted their quiet moment. Jean-Pierre appeared, his face marked with a mixture of exhaustion and determination. He hesitated, as though sensing the weight of their conversation.

"Am I interrupting?" he asked.

Genevieve smiled warmly. "Not at all. Come, sit with us."

As Jean-Pierre joined them, Genevieve reached for his hand. "There's something I want to share with you. It's about your grandparents and the choices they made during the war."

Jean-Pierre's eyes widened with curiosity. "I'd like to hear it."

And so, under the starlit sky, Genevieve began to recount the stories of her parents' bravery and sacrifices. She spoke not only of their actions but also of the emotional toll it took on them and their family. She shared their fears, their hopes, and their unwavering belief in doing what was right, even in the face of unimaginable danger.

As she spoke, Jean-Pierre listened intently, his expression shifting between admiration and reflection. When she finished, he sat silently for a moment, as though absorbing the weight of her words.

"Thank you for telling me this, *Maman*," he said finally. "It means more than I can say."

Genevieve squeezed his hand. "Remember, Jean-Pierre, you carry their legacy, but you also have your own family to protect. Whatever you choose to do, let it be guided by both courage and wisdom."

Jean-Pierre nodded a newfound resolve in his eyes. "I will."

As the night deepened, the three of them sat together, united by their shared history and an unbreakable bond.

And for the first time in weeks, Genevieve felt a glimmer of hope, that as one, they would find a way through the storm.

Chapter 31

Jean-Pierre gripped the aged map tightly, the faint scent of musty parchment and ink wafting upward as he traced the route marked upon it. The map, uncovered amidst the documents in the vault, was a revelation. Faded but still legible, it indicated a remote location deep within the mountains, a place Jean-Pierre had never heard mentioned before. His pulse quickened. This was no ordinary artefact; it was a doorway to the past, perhaps even the key to understanding Louis Dupont's and Jacques Lambert's wartime roles.

Early the next morning, Jean-Pierre packed supplies, including a flashlight, a sturdy pair of boots, and a journal. He informed his family of his plan, though he omitted the specifics, not wanting to alarm them. Adrien offered to accompany him, but Jean-Pierre insisted on going alone.

"This is something I need to see for myself first," he explained.

Genevieve's eyes lingered on him, a mixture of concern and pride. She said nothing, but her silent encouragement was unmistakable.

The journey to the marked location took him up winding mountain roads and into dense forests. As he approached the site indicated on the map, the terrain grew rugged, forcing him to park his car and proceed on foot. The forest was alive with the sounds of chirping birds and rustling leaves, yet an eerie stillness hung in the air as he ventured deeper. Sunlight filtered through the thick canopy above, casting dappled patterns on the ground. Jean-Pierre's heart pounded as he approached a clearing, where the outline of an old structure emerged from behind overgrown vegetation.

The base was hidden well, a testament to its purpose during the war. It was little more than a cluster of stone buildings, now weathered and crumbling, their walls entwined with ivy and moss. Jean-Pierre's breath caught as he stepped closer, the weight of history pressing down on him. This place, he realised, had once been a sanctuary for those fighting against oppression, a hub of clandestine activity.

Inside the first building, the air was damp and carried the faint scent of decay. The dim light barely illuminated the room, but Jean-Pierre's flashlight revealed what the years had concealed: crates stacked against the walls, some still sealed, others spilling their contents. He moved cautiously, brushing away cobwebs and debris, his eyes scanning for anything of significance.

One crate contained old uniforms: their fabric moth-eaten but still bearing the insignia of the Resistance. Another held rusted weapons and ammunition, reminders of the life-and-death struggles fought here. But it was a locked chest in the corner that drew Jean-Pierre's attention. The lock was rusted, but with some effort and the aid of a crowbar he found nearby, he pried it open.

Inside were items that made his breath hitch: a journal, meticulously written in Louis Dupont's handwriting, and a stack of letters tied together with twine. Each page seemed to vibrate with the emotions of its writer, recounting missions, strategies, and personal thoughts. Jean-Pierre's hands trembled as he lifted the journal and began to read.

The entries painted a vivid picture of a man caught in the storm of war. Louis detailed his collaboration with Jacques Lambert, their shared resolve to undermine the enemy, and the risks they took to save lives. Yet, what struck Jean-Pierre most was the raw honesty in the words. Louis wrote of his doubts, the moral quandaries that plagued him, and the guilt that lingered over the lives lost despite their efforts.

One entry stood out:

June 14, 1944

Jacques and I delivered the refugees safely to the border today. The operation was a success, but the cost weighs heavily. A mother and her child didn't make it. The checkpoint was more heavily guarded than we anticipated. Jacques blames himself, though it was I who insisted we press on. Can we call this a victory when innocent lives are the price?

Jean-Pierre's throat tightened as he imagined his grandfather's anguish. The lines blurred between heroism and tragedy, between right and wrong. This was not the black-and-white tale he'd heard in passing as a child. This was the complexity of war, of humanity.

The letters revealed another layer of the story. Many were addressed to Louis's wife, revealing his yearning for home, his love for his family, and his resolve to create a better future for them. Others were directives from Jacques Lambert, detailing missions and objectives. These letters hinted at Jacques's dual roles, as both a leader within the Resistance and someone with connections to shadowy networks that even Louis questioned.

June 20, 1944

Jacques insists on meeting with 'the others' to secure additional resources. I do not trust these men, but Jacques is unwavering. He believes their support is essential to the success of our mission. I fear he underestimates the cost of aligning with them. I must tread carefully, for the sake of our cause and our souls.

Jean-Pierre's thoughts raced. Who were these 'others?' Could they be connected to the modern threats his family now faced? He photographed the letters and journal pages, knowing he would need help deciphering their implications.

As the sun began to set, Jean-Pierre stepped outside, the cool mountain air grounding him. The base felt alive with ghosts, their stories demanding to be heard. He gazed out at the horizon, the majestic Alps bathed in hues of orange and pink. A sense of responsibility settled over him. This legacy was not just a chapter in his family's history; it was a thread woven into the fabric of who they were.

He was about to leave when he noticed a metal box partially buried near the edge of the clearing. Digging it out, he found more documents and a faded photograph of Louis and Jacques, their faces solemn but resolute. In the background, a symbol was scrawled on a wall—one he recognised from the earlier threats: the mark of the shadowy group opposing his investigation.

Jean-Pierre's chest tightened. The past and present were colliding in ways he hadn't anticipated. He realised now that uncovering the truth wasn't just about honouring his ancestors; it was about protecting his family from forces that had lain dormant but were far from extinct.

As he made his way back through the forest, the map and artefacts safely packed, his mind churned with questions. Who were the 'others' Louis had mentioned? How deep did Jacques Lambert's connections go? And how far was this shadowy group willing to go to keep the past buried?

When Jean-Pierre arrived home, the sight of his family waiting for him on the porch brought a bittersweet smile to his face. Ana's beautiful warmth, Genevieve's knowing look, Marcel's steady presence, Chantelle's quiet concern, and the children's unbridled joy reminded him of what he was fighting for.

He vowed silently to see this through—to honour the sacrifices of the past and ensure a safe future for those he loved.

Chapter 32

The early morning sunlight streamed through the wide windows of the château, bathing the vineyard in a warm glow. Jean-Pierre stood at the edge of the vineyard, surveying the rows of vines that had become a testament to his family's dedication and history. Today was a significant day as he hoped to taste the first samplings of his special vintage. The idea had been formed at the early stages of his ancestral project where he so carefully tended to the older vines in his vineyard. His idea was to create a wine to honour the legacy of Louis Dupont and the French Resistance, a Cabernet Franc named *"Résistance."*

As he strolled through the vineyard, Jean-Pierre let his hands brush against the leaves, the feel of the vines grounding him. Each cluster of grapes carried with it a story—a narrative of soil, sun, and care. And it was this vintage, he had decided, that would tell a deeper story.

He paused by one of the oldest vines, a gnarled plant that his great-grandfather Charles had once nurtured. The symbolism was undeniable. The FR in Cabernet FRanc would serve as a double entendre, representing both the grape variety and a tribute to the

French Resistance, their coded communications, and the resilience it took to endure the trials of war.

Jean-Pierre walked into the cellar, where Adrien and Ana were already waiting. The smell of oak barrels and fermenting grapes filled the air. Adrien, clad in jeans and a work shirt, grinned at Jean-Pierre. "So, this is it? The big project?"

Jean-Pierre nodded, a faint smile tugging at his lips. "This is more than a project, Adrien. It's a tribute."

Ana, standing by a table lined with tasting glasses and notes, tilted her head. "It's beautiful, Jean-Pierre. But how do you ensure this vintage stands out? How do you infuse the meaning you want it to carry?"

Jean-Pierre gestured to the barrels. "I started with the best grapes from the oldest vines. Grapes that have weathered storms, just like the people we're honouring. I've aged it in barrels that have been toasted to bring out notes of smoke and spice, symbolising the fire and grit of resistance fighters. And I've blended it carefully, ensuring every sip carries a balance of strength and elegance."

Adrien picked up a glass and swirled the wine inside. "So, every bottle tells a story?"

Jean-Pierre met his gaze. "Exactly. Every sip should remind the drinker of sacrifice, fortitude, and hope."

***

As the day wore on, the family joined Jean-Pierre in the vineyard. Chantelle and Adrien's children, Giselle and Pascal, ran among the rows, their laughter echoing like music. Marcel and Genevieve arrived, their presence adding gravity to the moment. Marcel carried a notebook filled with sketches and ideas for the label design, while Genevieve brought a basket of freshly baked bread and cheese for a shared lunch.

"Have you decided on the label?" Marcel asked, setting the notebook on the table.

Jean-Pierre nodded. "I want something understated but powerful. The name '*Résistance*' in bold letters, with an emblem of intertwined vines and a flame. It should evoke the courage of those who came before us."

Genevieve's eyes softened. "It's perfect. Your grandfather would be proud."

The family sat together in the vineyard, sharing a simple meal. Jean-Pierre looked around at their faces, each one carrying the weight of their shared history in different ways.

***

Weeks later, the batch of *Résistance* had progressed and was ready for further tasting. Jean-Pierre invited the family to the cellar, where he had arranged a small gathering. The oak barrels, now emblazoned with the name of the vintage, stood like sentinels guarding their contents.

As he poured the deep crimson liquid into glasses, the room grew quiet. The wine's aroma filled the space—a blend of blackcurrants, tobacco, and a hint of smokiness. Each family member took a glass, their expressions contemplative.

Marcel raised his glass first, studying the wine against the light. "It's more than a drink," he said. "It's a legacy."

Adrien took a sip, his eyes widening. "You've outdone yourself, Jean-Pierre. This is remarkable."

Ana, her voice filled with emotion, added, "It's like tasting history. You can feel the story in every note."

Even the children, given a small taste of grape juice to mimic the ritual, clinked their glasses with delighted giggles.

***

The official launch of *Résistance* took place in the château's grand hall, where Jean-Pierre had arranged a small gathering of local winemakers, historians, and friends of the family. The room was adorned with vintage photographs of Louis Dupont and other Resistance fighters, alongside displays of documents and artefacts Jean-Pierre had uncovered.

Standing at the front of the room, Jean-Pierre addressed the crowd. "This wine is more than a blend of grapes. It is a tribute to those who risked everything for freedom. It is a symbol of resilience, a reminder that even in the darkest times, the human spirit can endure."

The applause that followed was thunderous, filling the hall with a sense of unity and shared purpose. As the guests sampled the wine, Jean-Pierre felt a deep sense of fulfilment. *Résistance* was not just a product of his family's vineyard but a bridge between the past and the present, a way to honour the sacrifices of those who had come before while inspiring future generations.

Late that evening, as the festivities wound down, Jean-Pierre found himself alone in the vineyard under a canopy of stars. He held a glass of *Résistance*, the cool night air carrying the scent of earth and leaves. Marcel joined him, placing a hand on his shoulder.

"You've done something remarkable here, son," Marcel said. "You've shown that the past isn't just a shadow—it's a guide."

Jean-Pierre nodded; his gaze fixed on the vines. "I just hope I've done them justice."

"You have," Marcel replied. "And you've ensured their sacrifices will never be forgotten."

As they stood in silence, the glass in Jean-Pierre's hand felt heavier, as if carrying the weight of generations. But it was a weight he was proud to bear, knowing that in every bottle of *Résistance*, the Dupont legacy lived on.

Mario Zatta

Chapter 33

The dimly lit office in the Hôtel de Ville cast long shadows across the polished oak table. Mayor Robert Garnier sat at the head, fingers drumming against the wood, his sharp eyes scanning the two men seated across from him. Gaspard and Léo, his trusted enforcers, were men of few words but great efficiency. They knew how to intimidate without leaving a trace, how to apply just the right amount of pressure to make a problem disappear without it ever being linked back to Garnier.

Tonight, however, the mood was different. There was something more dangerous at play than a simple nosy historian. The mayor leaned forward; his voice calm yet laced with steel.

"I have received word that *Les Gardiens de l'Histoire* are aware of our young friend Jean-Pierre Dupont and his research."

Gaspard exhaled sharply through his nose, while Léo tilted his head in mild surprise. The name carried weight. *Les Gardiens* were a clandestine organisation, an old but elusive society that had long ensured certain historical truths remained buried. Their motivations aligned with Garnier's own, though their methods were far more extreme.

"This is fortuitous for us," Garnier continued, a slow smile creeping across his face. "It appears that they have taken matters into their own hands."

Léo shifted in his seat. "So, they're putting pressure on him too?"

"Indeed," the mayor replied, steepling his fingers. "And from what I understand, their threats carry more weight than ours ever could. It seems young Dupont has unknowingly stumbled into a nest of vipers."

Gaspard grunted. "If *Les Gardiens* want him silenced, we might not need to lift a finger."

Garnier nodded approvingly. "Precisely. Our work is being done for us, without us getting our hands dirty."

There was silence as they each contemplated the implications. The mayor's political influence depended on maintaining control, on ensuring that certain historical events remained forgotten. If Jean-Pierre uncovered the truth about the land disputes, the corrupt wartime deals, and the families who had been wronged, it could spell disaster.

"Then what's our next move?" Léo finally asked.

"For now, we watch," Garnier said smoothly. "We let *Les Gardiens* apply the pressure. If they succeed in silencing him, all the better. If he proves more resilient, then we step in. But not before."

Gaspard smirked. "Less work for us."

"Exactly." The mayor's eyes gleamed with satisfaction. "Let them do the dirty work. If anything happens, we had no part in it. No connections. No involvement."

He leaned back in his chair, exhaling contentedly. "And if they fail…" His gaze darkened. "Then we will ensure Jean-Pierre Dupont learns what happens to those who dig too deep."

The meeting continued late into the night, detailing contingency plans and possible avenues of intervention. But for now, the mayor was confident. The perfect storm was brewing around Jean-Pierre, and he didn't even see it coming.

Mario Zatta

Chapter 34

The sun dipped below the horizon, casting long shadows across the vineyard as Jean-Pierre stood outside the château, reviewing the documents he had unearthed. That final clue—the map and the series of notes that brought him closer than ever to unravelling the full truth of Louis Dupont's wartime heroics. Wass this all of it? He was so engrossed that he didn't hear the sound of approaching footsteps until it was too late.

"Jean-Pierre Dupont," a voice called from the darkness.

Jean-Pierre turned sharply, his heart racing. Three men emerged from the shadows. Their tailored suits contrasted sharply with the rugged terrain of the vineyard, but their demeanour was unmistakably menacing. The man in the centre, tall and stern-faced, stepped forward. His piercing eyes locked onto Jean-Pierre's.

"We warned you," the man said, his tone icy. "But you've persisted."

Jean-Pierre squared his shoulders, refusing to show fear. "Who are you?" he demanded. "What gives you the right to threaten my family?"

The man's lips curled into a cold smile. "We are *Les Gardiens*. We exist to protect a legacy—a legacy that does not belong to you alone. Your investigation threatens to expose secrets that were never meant to see the light of day."

"Secrets?" Jean-Pierre's voice rose. "You mean the truth about my grandfather and the Resistance? What harm could that possibly do now?"

The man's expression darkened. "You're naive if you think this is just about history. The actions of your ancestors and Jacques Lambert were not without consequences. There are powers—governments, and organisations—that have an interest in keeping certain details buried. Your persistence jeopardises more than just your family's safety."

Jean-Pierre clenched his fists. "So you're saying I should just walk away? Pretend none of this ever happened?"

"Exactly," the man said, his voice hard. "This is your final warning. Cease your investigation, destroy the documents, and let the past remain in the shadows. If you refuse..." He paused, letting the unspoken threat hang heavily in the air. "You've already seen what we're capable of."

Jean-Pierre's mind raced. The tampered car, the strangers near the vineyard, the veiled warnings—it all led back to these men. For a moment, doubt crept into his resolve. Could he risk further harm to his family? Was the truth worth the cost?

But then he thought of Louis Dupont's courage, of the sacrifices made by the Resistance. He thought of his children's faces, their laughter, their future. No, he couldn't turn his back on this.

"I won't stop," Jean-Pierre said firmly, meeting the man's gaze. "This is my family's story. I have a right to know the truth."

The man's eyes narrowed. "Then you leave us no choice. The next time we meet, you'll regret it."

Without another word, the men turned and disappeared into the darkness, leaving Jean-Pierre alone with his thoughts. His legs felt weak, and he stumbled back against the stone wall of the château. He closed his eyes, taking a deep breath to steady himself.

Genevieve found him moments later, her expression a mix of concern and determination. "What happened?" she asked, placing a steadying hand on his arm.

"*Les Gardiens*," he said, his voice trembling slightly. "They confronted me. Gave me an ultimatum to stop the investigation."

Genevieve's eyes widened, but she quickly composed herself. "What are you going to do?"

Jean-Pierre looked at her, his resolve hardening. "I'm not giving up. But we need to be prepared. They won't stop at threats."

Marcel joined them on the terrace, having overheard part of the exchange. "Jean-Pierre," he said gravely, "if they're willing to go this far, we must consider the safety of everyone. This isn't just about you."

Jean-Pierre nodded. "I know, *Papa*. But this isn't just about me, either. It's about honouring what Louis, and the others fought for. If I back down now, what does that say about us?"

Marcel placed a hand on his son's shoulder. "Then we'll all face them, but we'll be smart about it. I'll contact the authorities again. If *Les Gardiens* want a confrontation, they'll find us ready."

Inside the château, Chantelle and Adrien were helping Ana prepare dinner. When Jean-Pierre entered the room, the tension in his shoulders was evident. Chantelle paused, studying her brother carefully. "What is it?" she asked quietly.

Jean-Pierre hesitated before recounting the encounter. As he spoke, Adrien's face grew grim. "These people sound dangerous," Adrien said. "We need to take this seriously, Jean-Pierre."

"We are," Jean-Pierre assured him. "But I can't stop now. Not when I'm so close."

Ana set down a bowl of salad and crossed the room to stand beside her husband. "We'll get through this," she said softly, her eyes filled with determination. "But promise me you'll be careful. The children need their father."

Jean-Pierre's heart ached at her words, but he nodded. "I promise."

That night, as the family gathered for dinner, the atmosphere was subdued but resolute. Marcel looked at them all, his voice steady. "To us," he said. "No matter what comes, we stand together."

For a moment, the weight of their struggles lifted. But as Jean-Pierre glanced around the table at the faces of those he loved, he knew the battle was far from over. *Les Gardiens* had made their move, but he wasn't backing down.

The truth—and his family—was worth fighting for.

Chapter 35

Marcel Dupont leaned back in his leather armchair, his eyes fixed on the stack of documents spread across the table before him. Chantelle sat opposite, her expression written with concentration as she sifted through the pages of notes and records, they had painstakingly compiled over the past few weeks. The weight of their discovery was palpable—*Les Gardiens*, the shadowy group threatening their family, was not as unified as it seemed.

"Look at this," Chantelle said, pushing a document towards her father. Her finger tapped a highlighted section detailing internal correspondence within *Les Gardiens*. "This mentions disagreements among the leadership about how to handle 'legacy investigations.' Some of them didn't agree with the threats."

Marcel adjusted his glasses and read the passage carefully. His mind, sharp despite the years, began piecing together a strategy. "If there are fractures within their ranks, we may have an opportunity," he said, his voice calm but resolute. "Divide and conquer. We've always been stronger when the opposition is distracted."

Chantelle leaned forward; her tone cautious but hopeful. "Do you think we can use this to negotiate? To get them off our backs?"

Marcel's lips pressed into a thin line. "Negotiation might be our best option. But it has to be handled delicately. If we misstep, it could escalate their aggression."

They spent the next few hours poring over the documents, identifying key figures within *Les Gardiens*. One name stood out—Michel Vasseur. He appeared to be a high-ranking member who had expressed dissent in several of the internal correspondences. If anyone could be swayed to their side, it was him.

***

The following evening, Marcel and Chantelle found themselves in a quiet café in Geneva. The location had been chosen for its anonymity—a place where strangers could meet without drawing attention. Michel Vasseur had agreed to meet after receiving a carefully worded message from Marcel, one that hinted at shared interests without revealing too much.

As they waited, Chantelle glanced around nervously. "Do you think he'll come?"

Marcel nodded. "If he's as conflicted as his correspondence suggests, he'll want to hear what we have to say."

Minutes later, a tall man in his late fifties entered the café. His sharp eyes scanned the room before settling on Marcel and Chantelle. He approached their table with measured steps, his expression guarded.

"Monsieur Dupont," Vasseur said, his voice low. "You've been persistent. I hope this meeting is worth my time."

Marcel gestured for him to sit. "Thank you for coming, Monsieur Vasseur. We're here because we believe there is a path forward that benefits us both."

Vasseur raised an eyebrow but took a seat. "I'm listening."

Chantelle spoke next, her voice steady despite her nerves. "We've uncovered evidence of internal disagreements within *Les Gardiens*. We know not everyone supports the threats against families like ours."

Vasseur's eyes narrowed. "You've been digging deeper than you should."

"Only to protect our family," Marcel interjected. "We're not looking to expose anyone or disrupt the organisation. But we can't ignore the threats. We believe you might feel the same."

Vasseur leaned back, his expression unreadable. After a moment, he said, "And what do you propose?"

Marcel chose his words carefully. "A truce. We halt our investigation, and in return, your group leaves us in peace. We're not your enemies, Monsieur Vasseur. We're just a family trying to understand our legacy."

The room seemed to hold its breath as Vasseur considered their proposal. Finally, he nodded slowly. "I can't promise anything on behalf of the entire organisation, but I can bring this to those who share my concerns. Perhaps we can reach an understanding."

Chantelle's shoulders relaxed slightly. "Thank you. That's all we're asking for."

***

Over the next few days, Vasseur's influence within *Les Gardiens* became apparent. The threats ceased, and the oppressive presence that had loomed over the vineyard seemed to dissipate. However, Marcel knew better than to assume the danger had passed entirely.

One evening, as the family gathered in the study, Marcel shared the developments with them. "We've bought ourselves some time, but we must remain vigilant. *Les Gardiens* is not a group to underestimate."

Jean-Pierre, who had been quiet throughout the discussion, finally spoke. "Do you think they'll keep their word?"

Marcel met his son's gaze. "I believe Michel Vasseur will try. But trust is not something we can afford right now. We need to proceed with caution."

Chantelle added, "At least we've shown them we're not easily intimidated. That counts for something."

Genevieve placed a reassuring hand on Jean-Pierre's shoulder. "We've said we will get through this, and we will, as we always have."

As the family sat in silence, the weight of their shared struggles hung in the air. Yet beneath it all was a sense of unity—a determination to protect their legacy and each other, no matter the cost.

Chapter 36

Jean-Pierre stood before the heavy oak doors of the town hall, his father Marcel at his side. The late afternoon sun bathed the square in a yellow hue, but the warmth did little to calm the storm of emotions within him. This was it—the culmination of months of investigation, countless sacrifices, and hard-earned revelations. The story of Louis Dupont and his role in the Resistance would finally be laid bare. The challenge now was to tell the story with care, respecting both the heroism and the moral ambiguity of his ancestor's choices.

Marcel placed a reassuring hand on Jean-Pierre's shoulder. "You've done well, son. Today, we honour our family and ensure their legacy is preserved with integrity."

Jean-Pierre nodded, drawing strength from his father's presence. Together, they pushed open the doors and entered the hall, which was filled with local historians, community leaders, and members of *Les Gardiens de l'Histoire*. The atmosphere crackled with anticipation and an undercurrent of scepticism.

At the front of the room, a large table was covered with artefacts: faded documents, maps, photographs, and the personal effects of Louis Dupont. A projector cast a sepia-toned image of Louis onto the wall behind them—a young man with determined eyes and a strong jaw, his gaze unwavering even in the face of unimaginable peril. At the back of the room, Gaspard and Léo sat innocuously as silent observers, hidden among the audience.

Jean-Pierre began, his voice steady despite the weight of the moment. "Thank you all for coming. Today, we share a story that has remained hidden for decades—a story of bravery, sacrifice, and the complex choices made during one of history's darkest chapters."

He gestured to the map spread across the table. "This map, along with the documents we've recovered, details a daring rescue operation carried out by my grandfather, Louis Dupont, in collaboration with Jacques Lambert and other members of the French Resistance. Their mission was to save a group of political prisoners from certain death, risking their lives to fight for freedom and justice."

As Jean-Pierre spoke, Marcel stepped forward, pointing to key locations on the map. "The operation, codenamed *Ciel Clair*, involved coordinating intelligence from within occupied territories, securing safe houses, and executing a carefully timed ambush on a convoy transporting prisoners. It was an extraordinary feat of bravery and strategic acumen."

Jean-Pierre continued; his voice tinged with emotion. "But Louis's actions were not without cost. In the chaos of war, he faced impossible choices—choosing whom to save when resources were scarce, prioritising missions that would yield the greatest impact, even if it meant leaving others behind. These decisions haunted him, yet he carried them out with unwavering resolve, believing in the greater good."

The room was silent, the gravity of the story sinking in. Jean-Pierre scanned the faces of the audience, noting the mix of admiration and sombre reflection. He knew that while heroism was celebrated, the moral complexities of war often left scars that were difficult to reconcile.

Marcel stepped back to let Jean-Pierre address the more personal aspects of their findings. "Louis Dupont was a hero, but he was also a man—flawed, burdened by the weight of his choices, and deeply committed to his cause. Through his letters, we've come to understand the inner conflict he faced. He wrote about the lives he couldn't save, the comrades he lost, and the toll it took on him and those he loved."

Jean-Pierre paused, his voice breaking slightly. "He also wrote about his family—about the vineyard that gave him solace, the hope that one day, he could return to a world where his children and grandchildren would live in peace. That hope kept him going, even when the odds were against him."

Marcel added, "Louis's story is a testament to the resilience of the human spirit. It reminds us that history is not black and white but filled with shades of grey. Our responsibility is to honour his legacy by acknowledging both his triumphs and his struggles."

The presentation concluded with a moment of silence, allowing the audience to absorb the weight of what had been shared. Then, one by one, members of the audience began to speak—sharing their reflections, asking questions, and expressing their gratitude for the Dupont family's dedication to uncovering the truth.

An elderly historian stood, his voice trembling with emotion. "As a custodian of our local history, I thank you for shedding light on a chapter that deserves to be remembered. Louis Dupont's actions remind us of the courage and sacrifice required to preserve our freedoms."

Even a representative of *Les Gardiens*, who had initially opposed the investigation, stood to address the room.

"While we may have had our differences, I cannot deny the importance of this work. The truth, as complex as it may be, deserves to be told. The Dupont family has honoured their legacy with dignity and courage."

After the event, Marcel and Jean-Pierre lingered in the empty hall, their hearts full but their minds still reeling from the day's events. Marcel turned to his son, his expression a mix of pride and solemnity.

"You've done something remarkable, Jean-Pierre. Louis would be proud."

Jean-Pierre nodded; his gaze fixed on the photograph of his grandfather. "I just hope I've done justice to his memory—and that we've shown the world the strength of our family's legacy."

Marcel placed a hand on Jean-Pierre's shoulder, his voice steady. "You've done more than that. You've reminded us all of the importance of perseverance, fortitude, courage, and the pursuit of truth."

As they left the hall and stepped into the cool evening air, Marcel looked up at the starry sky, feeling a profound connection to the past and an unshakable determination to carry its lessons forward. Jean-Pierre, looking at his father, followed his gaze to the heavens.

***

Back at the château, the family gathered in the living room, their faces glowing with pride and relief. Genevieve poured glasses of wine, raising hers in a toast.

"To Louis Dupont and the legacy he left us—to perseverance, courage, and the strength of family."

The glasses clinked, and for a moment, the weight of the past lifted, leaving only the warmth of their shared bond.

Jean-Pierre sat back, watching his family, his heart full. The journey had been long and arduous, but it had brought them closer together, forging a connection that would endure for generations.

As the evening drew to a close, Marcel leaned over to Jean-Pierre, his voice low but firm. "This is just the beginning, son. The past is always with us, but it's how we carry it that defines us. And you've shown that we carry it with honour."

Chapter 37

The sun dipped low over the sprawling Dupont vineyard, casting its warm glow on the vines that stretched as far as the eye could see. The warm, late summer air carried the scent of ripe grapes and freshly cut grass, mingling with the soft hum of conversation and the gentle clinking of glasses. Family and friends gathered under a canopy of twinkling string lights, their faces alight with laughter and camaraderie.

Jean-Pierre stood at the edge of the gathering, watching the scene unfold. His children, Giselle and Pascal, darted between the rows of vines, their laughter ringing out like music. Pascal held a small wooden sword, proclaiming himself a knight, while Giselle pretended to be a queen, her crown fashioned from grape leaves. The sight filled Jean-Pierre with a profound sense of peace and hope, a stark contrast to the turbulent months that had brought them to this moment.

Genevieve moved gracefully among the guests, her presence radiant as she refilled glasses and shared warm smiles. She was the heart of the gathering, ensuring everyone felt welcome. Marcel stood near the centre, holding court with a group of family friends, his deep voice weaving stories of the vineyard's history and the Dupont legacy.

Chantelle and Adrien, seated at a rustic wooden table, were deep in conversation with Ana. The three of them laughed easily, the bonds of family strengthened by the trials they had faced together. Jean-Pierre caught Ana's eye, and she gave him a small, reassuring smile that warmed his heart. She had been his anchor through it all, her quiet strength and unwavering love reminding him of what truly mattered.

Nearby, the centrepiece of the evening stood proudly—a barrel of the newly bottled Cabernet FRanc, *Résistance*. The label, designed by Jean-Pierre himself, bore the name in bold, elegant letters, with the "FR" subtly capitalised to honour both the wine's origin and the French Resistance. It was more than just a vintage; it was a tribute to their ancestor Louis Dupont, to his courage, and to the strength of their family.

As the evening progressed, Marcel tapped his glass lightly, signalling for attention. The gathered crowd fell silent, their faces expectant as they turned towards him.

"My friends, my family," Marcel began, his voice rich and steady. "Tonight, we celebrate not just a vintage, but the strength of those who came before us. Louis Dupont faced unimaginable challenges during one of history's darkest times. His actions remind us that resilience is not just enduring hardships but rising to meet them with courage and conviction."

He gestured towards Jean-Pierre, who stepped forward, his heart pounding slightly as all eyes turned to him. "This journey began with a desire to understand our past," Jean-Pierre said, his voice steady despite the emotion welling within him. "What we discovered was not just a story of heroism but of complexity, sacrifice, and the enduring power of hope. Louis's legacy is not just his own—it's ours, carried forward in every bottle of wine we craft and every moment we share as a family."

Jean-Pierre raised his glass high, his gaze sweeping over the faces of those he held dear. "To resilience. To Resistance," he said, his voice strong. "To honouring the past, embracing the present, and building a future worthy of those who came before us."

The crowd echoed his words, "Resistance", their glasses raised high as the sound of the toast reverberated through the vineyard. The moment felt timeless, as though the spirit of Louis Dupont himself was present, smiling upon his descendants.

As the guests returned to their conversations and laughter filled the air once more, Jean-Pierre found himself drawn to the edge of the gathering. He watched his children play, their boundless energy and innocent joy a poignant reminder of what he was fighting to protect.

Genevieve joined him, slipping her arm through his as they stood side by side. "They're the future," she said softly, her voice filled with quiet pride. "And you've ensured that future is one they can embrace with pride and purpose."

Jean-Pierre nodded, his gaze never leaving his children. "I've learned that resilience isn't just about enduring—it's about building something better. For them. For all of us."

The two of them stood in silence for a moment, the vineyard stretching out before them, its vines a testament to generations of care and cultivation. The setting sun painted the sky in hues of amber and rose, a breathtaking backdrop for the celebration of life and legacy.

As the stars began to appear in the twilight sky, Jean-Pierre turned back towards the gathering. The warmth of his family's love and the strength of their shared history filled him with a renewed sense of purpose. Together, they had faced the shadows of the past and emerged stronger, united by their perseverance and bound by their shared legacy.

With a final glance at the horizon, Jean-Pierre smiled, his heart full.

The future awaited, and he was ready to face it with his family by his side.